# SANCTUARY

In the vast agricultural *cerrados* area of Brazil, Emily Noble, a children's book illustrator, wants to find her missing brother — a man who has been living a hidden life as a mercenary. She runs into danger when the trail leads her straight to Christovao Santos, the man who recruited her brother . . . All three have been targeted for death. All three have secrets. And the killer knows them all.

Books by Sharon K. Garner
Published by The House of Ulverscroft:

RIVER OF DREAMS
LOKELANI NIGHTS
THE SPANIARD'S CROSS

# SPECIAL MESSAGE TO READERS

This book is published under the auspices of

## THE ULVERSCROFT FOUNDATION

(registered charity No. 264873 UK)

Established in 1972 to provide funds for research, diagnosis and treatment of eye diseases. Examples of contributions made are: —

A Children's Assessment Unit at Moorfield's Hospital, London.

•

Twin operating theatres at the Western Ophthalmic Hospital, London.

•

A Chair of Ophthalmology at the Royal Australian College of Ophthalmologists.

•

The Ulverscroft Children's Eye Unit at the Great Ormond Street Hospital For Sick Children, London.

You can help further the work of the Foundation by making a donation or leaving a legacy. Every contribution, no matter how small, is received with gratitude. Please write for details to:

**THE ULVERSCROFT FOUNDATION,
The Green, Bradgate Road, Anstey,
Leicester LE7 7FU, England.
Telephone: (0116) 236 4325**

**In Australia write to:
THE ULVERSCROFT FOUNDATION,
c/o The Royal Australian and New Zealand
College of Ophthalmologists,
94-98 Chalmers Street, Surry Hills,
N.S.W. 2010, Australia**

Sharon K. Garner, a proofreader/copy editor and a former library cataloguer, has published several novels and numerous short stories for adults and children. She lives near a lake in Pennsylvania with her EMT/welder husband, who has learned not to twitch when asked such questions as, 'How do you disable a big piece of equipment?' or 'How long does it take to bleed to death?' Two cats, one that leads her life as though starring in a television commercial for cat food, the other as though life is going to sneak up and bite her, complete the household. In her spare time the author reads English mysteries and does walk aerobics, both on a regular basis. She's also been known to work as a temp to support her writing habit.

SHARON K. GARNER

◆

# SANCTUARY

*Complete and Unabridged*

## ULVERSCROFT
*Leicester*

First published in the
United States of America


First Large Print Edition
published 2006

G
Garner, Sharon K
Sanctuary

This novel i            ies, characters,
places and                product of the
author's in  CG    C450972051   ed fictitiously.
16.99

Copyright © 2004 by Sharon K. Garner
All rights reserved

British Library CIP Data

Garner, Sharon K.
    Sanctuary.—Large print ed.—
    Ulverscroft large print series: romance
    1. Brothers and sisters—Fiction 2. Mercenary
    troops—Brazil—Fiction 3. Romantic suspense
    novels 4. Large type books
    I. Title
    813.5'4 [F]

    ISBN 1–84617–287–X

C450972051

Published by
F. A. Thorpe (Publishing)
Anstey, Leicestershire

Set by Words & Graphics Ltd.
Anstey, Leicestershire
Printed and bound in Great Britain by
T. J. International Ltd., Padstow, Cornwall

This book is printed on acid-free paper

SOUTH LANARKSHIRE LIBRARIES

To Max,
with love,
for giving me the freedom
to live my dream.

# 1

'Please don't make me shoot you. I want nothing from you except information.'

Emily Noble's voice quavered. A fever had waylaid her about two hours ago, making her shoulders, her whole body, ache relentlessly. The old pistol she'd discovered in the rental car's glove box trembled in her grasp, before her brother's training kicked in. Heart racing, she brought up her left hand to steady the heavy gun.

A brief stillness, when he first saw the gun, was her only clue that she had shaken Christovao Santos. His military walk and his air of authority were familiar when he strode into the room where she lay in wait. Her father and her fiancé sported both in abundance. Her brother James had a mere hint of each.

The big Brazilian recovered and finished lighting a cigarillo. He studied her through its smoke, like she was a long column of figures that didn't quite add up. A look of watchful expectation replaced his wooden expression.

'Please. Put the gun down and we'll talk.' He spoke with a slight accent. 'A beautiful woman holding a small cannon plays hell with my concentration.'

Beautiful? He must be desperate, too. The last time she'd looked into a mirror, her left cheek had been a fading, glorious purple, and her blackened left eye had reached the yellow stage. The rest of her bruises, especially the emotional ones from the assault, didn't show, but they made their presence known in her fevered trembling and the cold sweat that drenched her anew when she first saw Christovao Santos. He filled the room with a dangerous presence as well as with his physical size.

And why didn't he stand still, damn him? How could he . . . waver like that?

She blinked, trying to clear her vision. 'Why don't you cut the crap and concentrate on what I'm saying. Where's my brother?' She scarcely recognized the cold, determined, faraway voice as her own. 'I'm dirty, drenched, and desperate. I'll ask nicely — once.'

'You forgot dangerous,' he said around the cigarillo.

The condescending sneer he'd pasted over his casual wariness vanished when she lowered her extended arms and fired a round into the hardwood floor between his booted feet. He was a cool one, she'd give him that.

2

He merely rocked back slightly on his heels.

'You're right. I forgot dangerous.' Recovering from the recoil, she pointed the gun at his chest while echoes of the small explosion reverberated in her pounding head. The acrid scent of gunpowder filled the eight feet of space between them, nauseating her.

Amused respect now gleamed in his violet eyes as they flicked from the marred wood at his feet to her perspiring face. 'I should probably ask. Who's your brother?'

'James. James King.' She gulped after the words, wondering if she was looking at the man responsible for James's disappearance, or at the man who might help her find him.

His even features tightened, carved into lines that were all business. 'Second mistake, *senhorita*. The first was coming here.' He buried the cigarillo upright in a sand-filled crystal bowl on the desk . . . and then he looked past her.

Did he really think she'd fall for that? She'd made sure she was in a defensible position in this office or study, with a wall behind her and the desk to dive behind for cover. This had been the only room in the house with a swath of light knifing from it into the soft Brazilian night.

The violet eyes were frosty now. 'Sami, the lady needs to lie down. Help her relax then show her to a room. She'll be staying with us until someone comes to claim her.' Then Christovao Santos stepped smartly aside.

She felt a warm touch, with moderate pressure, on the right side of her neck. At the same moment, a large, dusky hand and arm appeared over her left shoulder, catching the gun as it tipped forward out of her control and out of her grip.

Color faded from the room and from the cold face watching her. Christovao Santos grew steadily taller, wavering all the while, until he towered over her. Then she noticed the feathery grain of the tropical hardwood floor beside her nose. Before the curtain of darkness fully closed around her, she groaned with despair and regret. She had failed James — and she was going to die before she found out how Christovao Santos did that.

★　★　★

Emily bobbed to the surface of sleep, hungry and tucked up in the most comfortable bed she'd ever been in, despite the area near the foot where a dead weight pinned the bed-clothes tightly around her legs.

So this was heaven? She looked around the shadowy room. Somehow she had never imagined heaven decorated in shades of lavender and sage green, or with exquisitely carved antique furniture.

Then she remembered several facts at once. She was alive and a prisoner on Christovao Santos's farm in Brazil where she'd come for information about James. A dark-skinned doctor had helped her through her fevered travails, repeatedly asking her one question until the monotony of it drove her to verbally lash out at him. He had laughed, a full, rich baritone, at her angry response. She would never forget the question. *Who sent you here?*

Fully awake now, she wondered where Christovao Santos had gone. He'd been in the room every time she drifted in and out, whether the room was lit by the sun or by lamps. In fact, she'd gotten into the habit of looking for him before letting go and slipping into exhausted sleep again and again and again.

She felt the bedclothes relax around her legs and looked down over the sheet and light blanket covering her. Walking up the bed toward her was the most unprepossessing black, gray and white tabby cat she'd ever seen. Old and battle-weary, with the remnants of one dark ear in tatters, he trudged along beside her left leg, his progress marked by a deep, rusty, grating sound. A purr? This had to be a male. Only a male cat could reach this state of disrepair and old age with no grace at all.

'Hey, fella,' she rasped, her throat parched. 'I hope you're friendly.'

He was. He butted his head against her hand, chirruping all the while. She was happy to see that close up he was clean, sleek, and well cared for.

A clicking sound and a shadow against the louvered door, abruptly bright with fading daylight, commanded her attention. She quickly shaded her eyes with one hand against the onslaught of painful light.

She might have known. Although she now lay several feet above floor level, Christovao Santos would soon loom over her a second time, sans wavering, because he was slowly approaching her, much as the cat had done.

She was alert enough and well enough to study him, and woman enough to notice that his khaki pants and shirt skimmed his tall, solid, sturdy frame from his wide shoulders to his large brown boots. Espresso-colored straight hair lay thick, smooth, and neatly trimmed against his head.

His tawny features were as neat and orderly as his hair, wide-set violet eyes with dark, smooth brows, a nose with a narrow bridge, and lips . . . the upper one rose in two gently

6

chiseled peaks while the lower one was full and curved. High cheekbones and small ears that lay flat against his head completed the attractive yet dangerous-looking package.

This was where she had come in. If she were certain Christovao Santos was a good man, then the look of control and power on his face as he bore down upon her might inspire her with confidence. If she were certain that he wasn't, then that look might fill her with nervous terror. Since she didn't know what kind of man she was dealing with, she bluffed. She gingerly sat up, calmly pulled the bed pillows behind her back for support, and gathered the willing cat to her like a teddy bear. And hoped she didn't gibber in fear.

'His name is Gato. That's Portuguese for 'cat.' ' His voice, deep and soft, saying the innocent, unexpected words eased her fears that his nearness meant imminent danger. 'He's scarcely left your side since you were put into that bed. Before that, he never left mine while I was in the house. Do you mind?'

'*Him* I don't mind. What did you give me?' Her words dragged their feet through her dry throat.

'A little something to help you sleep off the fever. You had a nice, long rest.' From the fruitwood nightstand he picked up a glass of clear liquid with a bendable, red-striped straw in it and offered it to her. When she drew back, his lips thinned.

'Don't be a fool. This is just water.' He took a sip out of the glass then shoved it at her. 'Actually, we didn't have to give you much of anything. Do you remember? You collapsed with fever in my study after shooting at me. You wouldn't have been out more than a few minutes with Sami's initial help.'

'I don't believe you,' she croaked, although she took the glass and drank deeply.

'Then don't.' He studied her. 'But you were exhausted, mentally and physically, and ripe for any Brazilian bug you hadn't met yet. Your body took over when you didn't have enough sense to take care of yourself.'

'I was in a bit of a hurry to get here,' she snapped.

He paused, eyeing her like a fascinating, yet repulsive, new discovery under a microscope. 'So it appears. Sami says someone hit you. Did it happen to you in Brazil? Who did it?'

'Go to hell,' she said.

His striking eyes sparkled. 'That's what you suggested to Sami. Many, many times. I think you're the only one who has ever said that to him and lived.'

The memory of the contrast of dark,

determined face and gentle, ministering hands slammed into her. Her fear was back, in the wobble of her voice. 'I want to leave here. Now.'

He answered her with silence.

'You can't keep me here against my will,' she continued, giving voice to that particular fear.

'I think you'll find that I can and I will. Very easily.'

She clenched her fist in Gato's fur, earning a meowed complaint. She hastily smoothed his fur and his hurt feelings. As Gato relaxed again beneath her hands, she watched his master do the same. It rolled over Christovao Santos in a wave, making him look much younger and very tired.

'Have we mistreated you? Neglected your injuries? Have we beat you? Starved you?'

'Not yet, although I'm very hungry,' she conceded, watching him with deep suspicion.

With one hand, he dragged forward a heavy wing-backed chair then pivoted it on one of its front legs until it faced the bed. He folded himself down into it. 'Look, we won't get anywhere circling each other like this. I'll answer one of your questions then you'll answer one of mine.' It wasn't a request.

She stroked Gato and considered her options. She was in a house in the remote *cerrados* agricultural area of central Brazil with a man who might be responsible for James's fate — and now hers. Unless she was mistaken, she was wearing someone's T-shirt and nothing else. She had been ill, for days apparently, in a strange bed. It would behoove her to cooperate with this man and garner information from him while she was at it.

James's whereabouts and welfare were her highest priorities, she reminded herself. If she had to deal with the devil himself to find James, then she would do it. She jerked her head in agreement.

'You may go first,' he said when she didn't speak.

She swallowed her surprise. 'My brother has disappeared. Do you know where he is?' She watched for every nuance of expression. He didn't show any.

'No, I do not. You said you're looking for James King. I last saw him about six months ago.' He grinned, making her blink at the deep dimple that dove into his right cheek. 'See, that wasn't so bad. Shall we try again? What makes you think James King might be here?'

Wariness and indignation waged a battle within her and indignation won. 'That's two questions. And you don't believe James is my brother. I can hear it in your voice, in the way you say both his names to set him completely apart from me.' It would have been wise to stop then but she couldn't, although she did pause for another sip of water. 'I know who and what I am, but you're a stranger to me. I should doubt everything you say, not the other way around.'

He leaned forward in his chair and she jerked back against the pillows, wincing with pain when her left shoulder came in contact with the carved headboard. His eyes weren't sparkling now. They burned with cold purple flames.

'James King doesn't have a sister. I've known him across many years and several continents. He never once mentioned a sister to me.'

She'd known other men in her life like this one. Christovao Santos would respect and value courage over cowering, spirit over tears. So, she kept her voice level and forced her hands to still on his cat's back. 'James wouldn't. For some reason he never tells his business associates or friends about me.'

Her world-hopping engineer half brother was the only family she had left. He had always kept her away from his business and his friends, saying it was better that way but without giving any explanation. Until recently she'd thought it had to do with possible romantic entanglements. The last time they'd seen each other, when he came to visit her in the States six months ago, she had brought up the subject of him not owning her publicly as a sister. James had simply said that engineering was a dangerous business because of the antiquated methods of travel he sometimes had to use and the troubled countries he visited all over the world. But he'd also told her that if anything suspicious happened to him, she should look up Christovao Santos in Brazil. He'd even written down the address for her.

'James is my half brother. My name is — '

' — Emily Noble from upstate New York,' he finished for her, snagging her gaze and not letting go. 'It's on your passport, the rental car papers, half a book of traveler's checks, a credit card, and the ID tag on a very small carry-on bag. You travel light. Fake IDs are getting better and better.'

'Nothing is fake about me or my IDs, as you call them.'

'Noble and King? Surely you could have done better than that.' He said it through a sneer.

'I'm sorry you don't like them,' she said, her clenched jaws muffling the words. 'James and I do. It's a family joke between my brother and me about our mother being attracted to men with those last names. A delusions of grandeur kind of thing. My turn, I believe.'

The one thing she knew about James that frightened her unexpectedly jabbed at her now like a paper cut. As usual, she struck at the heart of her fears. 'I suspect that James has a secret in his past, a secret he won't share with me. I think it happened years ago yet it still gives him nightmares. He won't talk about it. Were you involved in it?'

Again, the only hint that she had hit a nerve was a sudden stillness, followed by his settling back in the chair, watching her. 'James and I served together in a . . . military operation.'

Disbelief was thick in her words. 'James was in the military while I was still in school in England, before our parents died. But why would that give him nightmares? He never saw action.'

'I said a military operation, not the military.' He ignored the question hovering on her lips and appeared to come to a decision. 'We found your rental car. With no luggage to speak of, you'll have to make do.'

She must have moved or tensed. Gato, disgusted with her, slid out of her grasp to curl up beside her, his tail briefly slashing like a furry whip. Without his comforting nearness, panic welled up within her, and she fought to keep it out of her voice.

'I refuse to stay here unless I choose to.' She eyed him. 'So, why haven't you called the police about me? I trespassed. I fired a shot in your general direction. Won't your life stand up to scrutiny by the law, Senhor Santos?'

She'd bet this man was a great poker player. His face was unreadable, but she sensed that behind the mask he was deciding how much to volunteer without giving anything away. Eventually, she got more than she expected, but the words came slowly.

'Some strange things have happened here recently, to me and to Abundancia, my farm. Your unexpected appearance is simply the latest. I'm not willing to invite the police into this until I locate James, talk to him, and we decide between us what the hell is going on.'

Tension flowed out of her, leaving her weak and trembling. So she hadn't made a mistake in coming here to help James. She'd got it right. Everything that had happened to James before he disappeared and to her since then was connected to something else, and Christovao Santos was in it up to his thick, dark, too-neat hair.

Taking a shaky breath, she asked, 'Why did James tell me to find you if anything suspicious happened to him?'

This time he let his surprise show. 'Did he? We've kept in touch. James is a friend.'

'And you were in the military together?'

'In a manner of speaking. Will you trust me enough, for his sake, to tell me your side of the story first? Why do you think James has disappeared?'

Before she could begin, she swallowed a lump in her throat as big as a fist. She used the time to scratch Gato behind the ears, reducing him to a limp, furry heap against her left thigh. Anyone who owned and obviously loved a cat like Gato couldn't be all bad. It was a beginning.

'James lives in London, so we talk a lot by phone and e-mail. He told me, jokingly I thought, that he had without warning become accident-prone. The first incidents happened in his block of flats and appeared to be accidents, like falling down the stairs. The hall light was out and James said something tripped him. Then the lift doors opened when the car wasn't there for him to step into. He was in mid-step, lost his balance, and almost fell into the shaft.'

She paused. 'After that, a man with a knife mugged him. James said he knew by the look in the man's eyes that he was going to use the knife, so James refused to cooperate and defended himself instead. A bobby was close

15

by and helped to scare off the so-called mugger. After that, someone tried to run him down as he crossed the street.'

Christovao Santos stretched out his long legs, crossing one booted foot over the other. 'Was he hurt in any of these incidents?'

She played with the top edge of the sheet. 'Just bruises and frustration. He wasn't taking it seriously, but I was worried about him. Shortly after he told me about the almost-hit-and-run, he stopped answering my calls and e-mails. His voice mail said he'd be out of London for a few weeks. When I couldn't reach him, I called his secretary at home. She said he phoned her late one night and ordered her to take a few weeks off with pay, that he was closing the office for a while and she shouldn't go near the place until she heard from him.'

'And you're sure he's not just off on a job somewhere?'

'I'm sure. Sometimes James is out of touch for a month or more, but this time the silence felt different. The police in New York *couldn't* do anything, and the police in London *wouldn't* do anything, so I flew to England and went straight to the flat.'

She clutched the sheet now. 'My timing was perfect or terrible, depending on your point of view. I walked in on two men who

16

were very neatly and very systematically searching the flat.'

He pulled his legs back and sat forward, his elbows on his knees, his gaze sharp. 'What happened? What were they looking for?'

Suddenly she was tired. She eased down on her spine, burrowing into the bed, while being careful not to disturb the cat beside her. 'They were looking for James.' She hesitated as something slid out of reach in her memory of that night. 'They were upset that they couldn't find him at the apartment. When I turned up, they decided to find out if I knew his whereabouts.'

'Your face? And you managed to get away from them?' He was skeptical and suspicious again, and he didn't bother to hide either in his words. He pushed himself to his feet, marched around the perimeter of the room, and came back to lean against one of the carved posters at the foot of the bed.

'This,' his gesture took her in from head to toe, 'is very well done. Sami tells me the bruising is real. Looks good. The fever must have been a real bonus.' His voice became soft and purring, much nicer than Gato's harsh rumble. 'Things can go smoother for all of us. I'll offer you protection from them. If you'll tell me who you work for.'

His last words were encased in steel.

# 2

Weariness and confusion washed over her in waves, and she put a hand to her forehead. What did he want from her now? Her thoughts slogged through something thick and lumpy, making it difficult to think.

'Who I work for? Well, I freelanced for a few lean years,' she began uncertainly, 'until I got my first contract with Tot's Press. After that I . . . ' She stopped and shot up against the pillows.

'Hey, wait a minute. What do you mean they made it look good?' A healthy dollop of anger blew away everything in its path. 'I earned every one of these bruises, because yes, I managed to get away from those horrible men.'

He didn't answer but his face wore a half-smile that she itched to slap aside. That insult would look much better under his right ear.

Her mind leapfrogged from one outrage to another. 'Who am *I* working for? Who are *you* working for? And I don't care how many questions I've just asked because this little game of Twenty Questions is over.' She

18

crossed her arms over her chest and glared at him.

He turned, reaching the door at the same time that she reached the conclusion their chat had been an interrogation and it was over.

'Now that you're well, you'll answer me or you'll answer Sami. Trust me, I'm much nicer.'

She threw back the sheet and light blanket, covering the sleeping cat, and jumped out of the bed. Too late she realized it was a grave error to thrust her abused body upright so quickly. She barely made it to the poster, still warm where he had leaned against the wood. She wrapped both arms around it and tried to hang on, grateful that the T-shirt hung to her mid-thighs. In two strides he was next to her. In one graceful motion, he swung her around, adding to her dizziness, and then up into his arms.

She snagged his violet gaze with hers and scooped up a fistful of his shirt to anchor herself amid the room's spinning. 'Where's my brother, Christovao Santos of the *cerrados*? When James told me to come to you if anything happened to him, he didn't say whether it was because he trusted you or because he thought you might be involved. Which is it?'

19

He exhaled on a sigh. 'I hope he trusts me, but I fear this might have something to do with me.'

She followed his gaze to her clenched fist, filled with his khaki shirt and quite a few chest hairs. Then, together, they looked at his tan, long-fingered hand stretched high along her bare left thigh. When their eyes sought each other's again, neither looked away. She realized, with a jolt akin to an electric shock, that she could get a good snuggle going in Christovao Santos's arms.

He broke eye contact first, swearing evenly, enthusiastically, and at length in Portuguese. 'I'll probably regret this but I'm starting to believe you.'

Her grasp on his shirt loosened, and, as she spoke, she busily patted flat the wrinkles she'd made in the cloth. 'Find James or help me find him, Senhor Santos. That's all I want from you, I swear. I have no agenda, no ulterior motive. Nobody sent me, unless you count James. I'm a children's book illustrator, not a spy or anything else you suspect me of — or expect from me.' She was babbling, so she caught her lower lip between her teeth to stop the rising flood of words.

His eyes were warm, alight with humor and something else, as he concentrated on her mouth. 'Trouble, Emily Noble, is what I expect from you, and I suspect that's exactly what I'll get.'

'What do you think has happened to James?' Her voice wobbled on his name.

'He could still be on the run or gone to earth somewhere by now, or he might be hurt. It's a big world for a man to lose himself in and I don't know where to start looking.'

She gasped as the possibilities paraded across her mind's eye for what felt like the thousandth time. 'But why? What do those men want? Are they connected with your trouble here? Please tell me what you think is going on. And what my brother is hiding from me. I know you know, and I can't bear not knowing.' She swept her hair off her forehead with her free hand, still hanging onto his neck with the other. 'I'm so hungry.'

He sighed, a man accepting his fate. 'Are you well enough to get dressed and come to the *sala*? You need to eat something. We'll talk over dinner.'

'I'm starving, now that you mention it. But get dressed in what?' He still hadn't moved to put her down and she didn't mind at all. 'I travel light, remember. I left home and London in a hurry. The airlines managed to lose the one bag I packed.'

'Oh, hell, I forgot.' His gaze flicked to the louvered closet doors then back to her. Pain passed through his violet eyes on a swift journey, trapped for a moment in anger. He gently dropped her onto the bed, pulled his shirt out of his pants, and started to unbutton it.

'It's clean, and I just showered,' he explained in a quiet voice.

Mesmerized, she watched his strip tease take place one button at a time two feet in front of her eyes. Smooth hair, interrupted by a long white vertical scar, grew thick and dark in a sweep across and down the center of his chest and midriff, narrowing to disappear into the belted waistband of his khaki pants. Her gaze followed its flow and she gulped, actually lifting a hand to trace the scar before she caught herself. When he shrugged off the shirt, her eyes flicked from one big shoulder to the other, measuring their width.

'Put this on over your T-shirt.' He dropped the warm shirt, smelling of his soap and of him, onto her knees. 'Your boots and socks are over there. They were the only outer articles of clothing you were wearing that survived your journey and Sami's search.' He paused. 'Will you be all right on your own?'

'I think so. And thanks for asking. I'm not dizzy now. If that changes, I'll sit down wherever I am and yell. Where's my carry-on?' At least she could brush her teeth.

'It's in the bathroom.' He indicated a door near the bed. 'Sami searched it rather enthusiastically, too, but you'll find every-thing you need.'

What Sami had done was destroy the bag. He'd opened all the seams, even those on the straps. The flat remnants were wrapped around her toilet items, hair dryer, and the change of underwear she'd thrown in because of her past experiences with airlines. The articles with her name on them, or her IDs as Christovao Santos had called them, were there, except her passport and her car keys. Her fists and jaws clenched in unison at this discovery.

She forgot her flash of anger and helplessness when she looked into the mirror above the pale lavender marble vanity. Her shoulder blade-length, white-blonde hair was a dirty, tangled mess, her green eyes were sunken and blood-shot, and her fading bruises . . . Well, everything stood out in contrast to them, skin, hair, eyes, even her teeth when she smiled to check again for chips.

After responding to Gato's insistent scratching and caterwauling request to enter, she locked the bathroom door behind them. Not that it would do any good if Santos or this Sami person decided to come in. She craved a hot shower. However, with the shower scene from *Psycho* playing in her head, she ran a bath instead, washing her hair in the tub water before she added bubble bath and climbed in. At least she could see them coming from the tub.

Gato sat on the porcelain edge of the tub, watching every move she made with such intensity that she paused and stared back. For one crazed, self-conscious moment, she covered herself and wondered if Christovao Santos could see what the cat was seeing.

She grinned at her foolishness, asking the tom, 'Are you a remote viewer in cat form, Gato? That thought makes me wonder what your master and his sidekick really gave me. And how much.'

She didn't linger in the warm, soothing water, drying herself with the vigorous use of a soft towel. As she blow-dried her hair, she studied the room. The bedroom color scheme carried over into the bathroom. That told her a woman was, or had been, in residence there on a semipermanent basis. Instinct insisted that it wasn't Christovao Santos's mother or sister, if he had one, who had decorated these rooms. And he didn't wear a wedding band. She wondered if he had shared the comfortable bed in the next room with the mystery woman.

When she sat down in the wing chair in the bedroom to lace up her hiking boots, she glanced at the louvered doors of the large closet. Unable to resist either the urge or her rampant curiosity, she flung them open. Her breath caught as she gaped at the exquisite women's clothing inside, proving her earlier speculations. Everything from sexy lingerie to business suits to kicky cocktail dresses in a dazzling array of colors hung from the rails. She pulled out a French terrycloth robe and looked at the size. The label was in Portuguese but it looked like it might fit her. She was ready to slip it on when she hesitated, remembering Christovao Santos's glance at the closet doors and the look of pain in his eyes afterward.

The robe went back into the spot she had taken it from. She wouldn't risk it. She wanted answers and, providing the answers were the right ones, possible help from this man. If he didn't care whether she wore these clothes, then he would have offered them for her use, instead of the shirt off his back. His uninvited guest showing up for dinner wearing something from this closet would surely antagonize him.

The *sala*, he'd said as he left her room. She had no idea what that meant in Portuguese, so she trailed after Gato when he sashayed through the doorway of the screened and louvered bedroom door, in hopes that he knew the way to this *sala*. The evening was warm and clear and she welcomed the fresh air, pulling it deep into her lungs. How many days had she lost to fever and to Christovao Santos's 'help,' she wondered?

Gato moved with purposeful little cat steps and gave the impression he knew where they were going, so she continued to follow him. They stepped off the covered, colonnaded tile walkway outside her door into the lovely courtyard. A tinkling fountain with a pond stood in its center, while colorful beds of tropical flowers and small trees outlined its perimeter.

She'd scarcely noticed any of this the evening she sneaked in. She remembered stumbling through a tall gate into this space and choosing the only room in the house that had lights glowing. It had required great effort at that point to put one foot in front of the other to reach it. Her almost nonexistent plan had deteriorated from there.

She took note now that the neat, one-story, inverted U-shaped house with its red tile roof enclosed this peaceful courtyard on three sides. A stucco wall and the wood gate closed off the fourth side. The house's roofline was set off by a walkway around the peak of the roof, enclosed by a fairly high wall, reminding her of an elaborate widow's walk. She wondered what its purpose was.

Gato moved toward the back section of the house, his striped, furry butt and upright tail leading her onward.

She looked more closely at the surface beneath her boots and saw a patterned sea of color. Every inch of the courtyard was paved with mosaics, some plain. Others were like those she'd glimpsed in Rio de Janeiro. Circles, swirls, and wave patterns in every color of the rainbow danced beneath her boots. For one dizzying moment she wanted to pirouette across them. With her general weakness and sickbed hangover, she was sure she'd end up in the fountain pond if she tried it just then.

Her stomach rumbled when she caught the scent of roasting meat, accompanied by the sounds of Latin music playing softly. She followed her nose and ears and feline guide across the remaining courtyard. Each sense, and Gato, led her up onto the walk again and straight to a set of screened double doors that stood open to the air. A wide fan of light poured across the tiles. She stepped into it.

'*Boa tarde*, Emily Noble.' Christovao Santos's soft, deep voice, wrapping itself around the soft Portuguese words, sent a chill scurrying up her spine. Holding a drink, he rose from a chair and leisurely surveyed her from her clean, shining hair to her scuffed, tobacco-colored boots. His eyes lingered an extra moment on her left thigh, purple and yellow from her knee to where his shirt began. His full lips thinned briefly into an angry line.

Shivering again in the warm air, she felt his gaze as if he had touched her. 'Good evening, Senhor Santos.'

She was glad to see he wore another khaki shirt, his casual dress probably in deference to her clothing. It wouldn't surprise her to hear that he dressed for dinner. She was certain, however, that his general neatness and military carriage would give him presence even if he were dressed in rags.

'Call me Chris. Everyone does.' He nodded toward the bar. 'Would you like something?'

Alcohol appealed to her at that moment, but until she was sure the Brazilian bug that had invaded her body had moved on to other unsuspecting visitors, she would forego her evening sherry.

'Information and help,' she answered evenly. 'And juice, if you have it.'

He slipped behind the bar. 'A woman who goes straight to the point. I like that. But we'll eat first then talk. It's early for dinner in

Brazil, but I'm sure you're very hungry.' He handed her a chilled glass of what looked like freshly squeezed orange juice.

'You're very right.' Taking a sip, then a deep drink of the heavenly mixed-fruit nectar, she looked around the huge room, part bar, part dining room, and part sitting room. 'What exactly is the *sala*?'

'In Brazil the *sala de estar* is the sitting room, but we simply refer to this whole room as the *sala*. This farmhouse was built to my mother's design and specifications many years ago here at Abundancia. The open floor plan and her placement of the sets of double doors help with ventilation.'

'It's lovely. *Abundancia*. Abundance?'

He raised his glass to her. 'Very good.'

The wall behind the bar, which served as a backdrop for her smiling host and keeper, riveted her wide-eyed attention. An impressive collection of spears marched in a staggered yet orderly display from ceiling to bar height.

He followed the direction of her stare. 'I traveled extensively in Africa.'

'I'll bet that one has a story behind it.' She indicated the showpiece, the most impressive spear in the collection. 'How can anything look so deadly yet so beautiful at the same time?'

The spear was crafted from wood and iron, both black with age. Brass wire woven in a design covered the joint where the deadly spearhead met the shaft. At the butt of the shaft, beads, charms, and one black feather dangled. The shaft itself was carved, almost geometrically, and some of the notches were smeared with red paint. The whole weapon looked heavy, balanced, and well-crafted.

'The spear belongs to Sami. It belonged to his father before him,' Chris answered in a monotone.

The question in her eyes met the 'don't ask' in his, backed up by the look on his face. With another shiver, she tore her attention away from the wall of weapons. 'I'm glad my father just left me his chess set.'

'Please. Sit down.' Keen interest shone out of his startling violet eyes. 'Do you play?'

She chose a brown chenille overstuffed chair in the conversation area. It sat at right angles to a sofa and a loveseat covered with a tapestry fabric woven in golds and tans. Her chair's mate sat opposite her. A large, low game table, also serving as a coffee table, roosted in the center of the grouping on a Berber area rug.

'My father taught me as soon as I stopped chewing on the chess pieces. My mother didn't care for the game.'

'Would you like to play later, if you're not too tired?'

She paused to study him a moment. The hint of eagerness in his voice made her wonder if he was lonely here. Then, in a frightening smack, it struck her that this man still held her in his absolute power, yet she knew next to nothing about him. Nobody knew she was here, in his house. Her mouth went dry at the thought.

'Let's make it interesting.' Her suddenly raspy voice focused his attention on her mouth. 'If I win, I can have my car keys and passport, both of which you misplaced while I was ill.' She watched his face closely for his reaction.

He shrugged and smiled, his dimple present and accounted for. 'Ah, my unfortunate memory.'

Fear and anger ran in tandem inside her. Before she realized what she was saying, she answered him with an earthy Anglo-Saxon word and immediately apologized.

His handsome features grew stern. 'I will ask again. Have we been unkind to you? Have we harmed you in any way?'

'And I will answer again, not yet.' She felt shame, briefly, for baiting him then reminded herself that he was a stranger.

'Emily, you are much safer here, for the time being. Now, stop this. Please.' The words were soft but something in his eyes snapped.

His calling her Emily inexplicably brought her close to tears, which was unusual for her. She decided she must have been sicker than she thought. The Brazilian bug that laid her low had a lot to answer for.

'All right, I'll stop. For now. But only for James's sake and because I'm not fighting fit yet.'

'*Madre de Dios*,' he muttered.

'But I have one question I feel compelled to ask.'

'Is there any way to stop you?'

'No. You and Sami aren't . . . crazy or anything, are you?' She was only half-joking, evidenced by the definite squeak in her voice and her gulp.

He gave a quick grin and the dimple dove into his right cheek. She blinked. Grinning was definitely an exercise he should practice every hour or so. Christovao Santos would never look completely harmless, but that dimple made him look less dangerous, more approachable, and eight years old.

'Some people have hinted that I am, including my father before he died, and my mother. I'm over it now, though. And Sami is sane, capable, and loyal.' His gentle humor calmed her. His next words reassured her. 'You have my word, as James's friend, that no one from this house will harm you.'

# 3

She drew in a deep breath of relief. 'Thank you, Chris. I needed to hear that.' Her smile trembled but held.

With the lightest of touches, he ushered her to the dining area where he pulled out one of the heavy, carved mahogany chairs for her. She stilled for a moment as he pushed in her chair, unsure whether or not his nose had touched her hair. She chalked up the sensation to her weakness and draped her napkin across her lap.

A large number of matching chairs marched around the perimeter of this part of the room. That meant a number of extension boards for the table were stored somewhere. Someone, at sometime, had entertained on a large scale at Abundancia. She wondered if it had been Chris's mother, wife, or the mystery woman.

'Being fair and fair-haired, you stand out like a beacon in this country,' he said as he turned to take his place beside her, at the head of the table. 'Did you stop in Rio on your way here?'

'I passed through. I came to Brazil to find

you, not to see the sights. But why do you ask?'

'A green-eyed, white-gold blonde would create quite a stir there.' His voice turned hard. 'Of course, you know that. Most beautiful women know the value of their looks, and make use of them.'

At that, one brow arched itself up her forehead. 'Spoken like a cynical male.'

'It's the observation of a cautious male. Please, tell me about your journey to Abundancia.'

'Well, I tried to mind my own business on my way here. I really did. But despite that I'm not at my best right now, I had a healthy taste of the die-hard spirit of Brazilian men while I waited in Rio for my flight to Brasilia. My bruises apparently made them think I like it rough. I've never been so imaginatively propositioned or had my backside pinched as often as I have here. And I include Italy and Italian men in that statement. The last leg of the trip was the worst, from Brasilia to Barreiras. I didn't dare stand up to go to the bathroom.'

He laughed aloud at that, a deep, warm, thrilling sound. 'I apologize for the inconvenience of my countrymen's enthusiasm, but I'm glad they upheld our reputation. In that context, your bruises do give you a certain

. . . provocative distinction.' His warm gaze told her that here was another Brazilian man who liked what he saw, fading bruises and all.

A young man with the dark, sultry good looks of many Brazilians appeared, bearing platters of food. She returned his proud smile when he served her appetizer with a flourish. Chris introduced him as Luiz.

He was well into his large slice of cold melon, and she into her tiny one, before Chris broached the subject that interested her above all others. 'I've put out some feelers about James, and I've set some things in motion,' he said. 'And I received an e-mail today that might interest you. I didn't read it until after you woke up. I've answered it.'

'You mean it was from James? Oh, thank you.' She couldn't hide the eager, grateful tone in her voice. 'How long — ?'

'I don't know. It was in a kind of code, but we're fairly sure it came from James. I hope you'll enjoy the safety and hospitality of Abundancia until he contacts me and tells me what to do with you.' He saw her mutinous look and added, 'I have information you do not have. If what I suspect . . . It wouldn't be a good idea to leave here, Emily.'

'So you've said, senhor,' she said with a meekness that brought his head up sharply. 'And what do you suspect?'

He ignored her question and instead adjusted the napkin on his lap with a snap. 'I'll ask you to remember the men in James's flat and the pain you suffered at their hands. I want your word that you won't attempt to run away.'

She was stunned into silence by remembering the men in James's flat, so she simply nodded, wide-eyed. Unable to hide her trembling hands, she was grateful when he sent the conversation in a new direction.

'I asked you to trust me once before under false pretenses. I apologize for that. But I ask you to trust me enough now to tell me about you and James.'

'What choice do I have?'

'You can refuse, but I hope you won't. As I said, he never mentioned you. Of course, I often see him in Rio where we're too busy chasing other men's sisters for him to talk about his own.'

Her hands steadied. 'You can't shock me by telling me about James and women. He talks to me as if I were a brother, and he's never held anything back if I asked, or at least I thought so until recently. When our parents died and he became responsible for me, that's when he began to keep me away from his work and the men he works with. I'm sure anyone who has glimpsed us together in

London thinks I'm James's mistress. I have to wonder if it's only that one area of his life he's never let me into.'

He studied her face and hair. 'You don't look like him, you know. There's no resemblance at all.'

She heard a remnant of doubt in his voice and couldn't really blame him. She and James were very different in appearance. James's hair was chestnut brown, his eyes were warm brown with green flecks, like his father's had been, and he was taller than her own five feet, seven inches.

'My father, who dabbled in antiques as a hobby, called us an unmatched set. James and I had the same mother, who was British. Her clear green eyes and pale blonde hair were my legacies. James looks like his British father, our mother's first husband, who died when James was tiny. My father was an American. I was born in the States, but we lived in England for many years. James is much more British than I am.'

His dimple danced. 'I've noticed. How many years between you?'

'Seven. I'm twenty-six and James is thirty-three. He claims I was an afterthought.'

She guessed he was near James's age. Tiny lines radiated around his eyes, but his dark, thick hair showed no signs of gray.

'Our mother and my father, James's stepfather, were killed in a car accident when I was sixteen. James was in the British Forces at the time, a Royal Engineer. He sent me to my godparents in the States, and I went on to art school there. Soon after, he started his own engineering firm in England.' She lapsed into silence at the flood of memories.

'Please, go on with your story,' he prodded, after Luiz served the main course.

She looked longingly at the roast beef on his plate, which he was smothering with a red sauce, then cut into her toast topped with a poached egg. 'Only if you'll tell me your life story when I've finished. I demand equal time from you.'

He hesitated. 'Fair enough. If you'll accept an abbreviated and censored version, until you know me a little better.'

She glanced up at him through her lashes. 'Agreed. You know the rest of mine already. My life was uncomplicated until a few weeks ago. I live in rural New York State. I'm a freelance artist and illustrator. For the past few years I've concentrated on illustrating children's picture books for Tot's Press.'

'Successful?' He stopped impaling vegetables on his fork and waited for her answer.

'Comfortable. And I love the work. I've received good reviews for the books I've illustrated. Everything is in a bit of an uproar there right now because the publisher, my boss, took a two-month leave.

'I visit James in London as often as I can, or at least I stay at the flat when I'm in London. He's seldom there. My mother left me the tiny cottage in Cornwall where she grew up and where we spent our summers. I rent it out now. It helps pay my house mortgage between books. But that cottage is my haven, my sanctuary, and my favorite place to work, although I can work anywhere that's peaceful and quiet. I'll probably build on to it and move to Cornwall eventually, since I have dual citizenship. My parents left the London flat to James.'

'And do you live alone in rural New York State and London and Cornwall?' He watched her closely.

They paused while Luiz served Chris cake with a cream sauce. He placed a saucer of egg custard in front of her. She used the time to gather her thoughts. She understood what Chris really wanted to know and wondered what it meant that he'd asked.

When Luiz withdrew, she met his gaze in the glow of the candles on the table. 'Yes, I live alone. I don't even have a cat, present company on loan excepted.'

Gato, never faraway from her, was under

the table near her feet, his idling purr an accompaniment to their meal.

'What, no romantic ties? A beauty like you?' His skeptical tone pushed her toward defense in the form of confession.

'I date. I was even engaged once.' Her voice faltered on the words. 'Because of my father's work as a civilian on military bases, James and I have lots of friends in the military. I'd known Geoff forever. Then, while I was in England once visiting James, Geoff and I saw each other in a different way. Our friendship caught fire.

'He was Special Forces, and he was killed. I discovered in the harshest way that friendly fire is an oxymoron and not friendly at all. I've trod cautiously around military types since then. I still have lots of male military friends, but I won't date them. Life is dangerous enough on its own without my putting my heart in harm's way.'

His next question shocked her into the present because of its utter unexpectedness. 'And what do you want out of life, Emily Noble, now that you tread cautiously around military types?' The look on his face alerted her that the question had surprised him, too.

She shrugged, smiling. 'I find I still want the same things I've always wanted. To make the world a little better for my having been in it. To win awards for my illustrations. To move to my mother's cottage in Cornwall and turn the loft into a studio. To marry and have babies someday. To live to be old with someone I love. How about you?'

Instead of answering, he pushed his chair back then helped her with hers. 'Let's move to the sitting area. We'll have our coffee there.' When they were settled, he took his time lighting a cigarillo, a cigarette wrapped in tobacco rather than paper, with an elegant, plain gold lighter.

'You didn't answer me,' she reminded him gently. 'It's your turn to bare your soul. That was the deal.'

Again, she saw sadness flit through his eyes as he tossed his lighter into the air with one hand and caught it again, without looking at it. 'I want to make Abundancia the gold standard by which modern *cerrados* farms are measured, even more so than it is now. The men who work Abundancia are retired or ex-soldiers from the Brazilian army. I'd like to give more of them a place here to live and work in peace. Like you, at one time I thought I would marry and have a family. Now, I tread cautiously around all women. I'm content to live my life, take my pleasure, and die quickly when the time comes.'

She wondered what part the woman whose

clothes still hung in his house had played in crushing that particular dream.

'I hope we both get what we want, but I suspect that, like me, you've learned that life doesn't come with guarantees. That was brought home to me quite forcefully at age sixteen. Tell me about James now. How did you become friends with him? What has he done — ?'

She stopped in mid-sentence when a large, regal, dark-skinned man glided into the room so smoothly and silently that he might have had wheels instead of feet. She remembered him well.

Sami nodded to her then deliberately moved to the bar area. Chris excused himself and followed. They held a whispered conversation in a language she didn't understand. She tried to avoid staring, but the sheer size and presence of the two men together drew her eyes again and again. When Sami turned to go, he flashed her a friendly smile. She blinked before smiling in return. His square white teeth made a startling contrast against his coffee-colored skin.

In a velvet voice, he said, 'I'm glad to see you're feeling better, miss.'

'Thank you. Y-you must be Sami.' She felt warmth climb up and out the neck of Chris's shirt to her cheeks.

He nodded and went out.

Chris returned to the sofa. 'My manners are appalling tonight. I apologize for not introducing you.'

'Oh, I'm sure Sami knows me quite well,' she said in a tight voice. 'I certainly remember him and his questions. Did, um, did he undress me . . . or did you?'

'No, Sami did not undress you.' He paused, watching her until her face felt like flames licked beneath her skin. 'I didn't either. My cook, Mei, had that pleasure and assisted you in other ways. Feel free to visit her in the kitchen to say thank you. She'll probably let *you* in. Any male, except Gato, is stopped at the door.'

'I can't believe you would allow someone to keep you out of your own kitchen.'

'I humor her,' he interrupted in a businesslike voice. 'As you'll discover when you're feeling better, she's a very good cook. Now, you were asking how I got to know James and what he's 'done.' He hasn't 'done' anything that I'm aware of. In fact, he helped save my life and the lives of several others under my command.'

'He fought? James was in combat?' Amazement and disbelief were equally thick in her voice. 'Where? When?'

'James wasn't meant to see combat, but,

yes, he fought and he fought well.' His features hardened before he looked away. 'I was an officer in the Brazilian Army when I was recruited by an international unit, one of those hush-hush outfits that no one believes really exists. After that, like you, I decided to go freelance. *Mercenario*, a mercenary soldier. I commanded a unit of my own handpicked men. Briefly. I don't know what I was thinking. That's when my mother and father told me I was crazy.'

He looked at her now, watching her face for her reaction. She didn't know what he saw written on her features, but it wasn't distaste. Surprise was there, certainly. And shock. And a dread of what was coming next, all overlaid by a frisson of fear caused by the man watching her when realization struck. She'd shot at this big Brazilian ex-mercenary, and his giant friend had knocked her out with a touch. She shivered before he spoke again.

He noticed the shiver and looked away. 'James and I met in a London pub. I was in England on business. A mutual friend, fresh out of the military, introduced us.

'We had a very productive discussion that evening. James needed money to start his own engineering firm, he was an engineer, and he was ex-military. I had my first operation coming up with one special position left to fill. I needed an engineer.' He shrugged.

'James was a mercenary soldier?' she said in a monotone. 'You recruited my brother for a mercenary operation?' Her voice rose on the last words.

His grimace was a travesty of his dimpled grin. 'No, I did not recruit your brother to crew for me. He talked me into taking him. These were handpicked men, as I said. I'd known James at that time for a mere few hours. Our friend vouched for him, and I needed that engineer. James fit the bill. He signed on as a civilian attached to my unit.'

Her mind reeled at the information she had to absorb about the brother she trusted and thought she understood. But her love for him remained unshaken. Guilt crept in when she wondered what part being responsible for her, orphaned at sixteen and thrust into his care, played in his decision to take that drastic step.

'You didn't tell me where.' Her throat was parched, so she sipped her coffee.

'Africa. To say the operation ended badly is an understatement. We were double-crossed by one of our own. I had a bullet in my chest and most of my unit was wiped out.'

Her cup clattered against the saucer when she set it down. 'James's nightmares?'

'Probably. It features heavily in mine. After that, I got out of the business. My father died shortly after I was fit to travel. My mother and Abundancia needed me. Sami and I have been here ever since. That's all you need to know about it for now.'

A tingle of fear zinged through her. 'And you think James's accidents and the men in his flat have something to do with that operation?' She paused as another piece clanged into place. 'You've had accidents yourself, haven't you? Is that why you thought someone sent me, to get close to you so they — he — could . . . ?'

'You're tenacious, aren't you?' He lit another cigarillo, looking at her with exasperation through its smoke. 'The survivors of my unit have stayed in touch with me and with each other. Five weeks ago, I started getting anonymous e-mail messages about their accidental deaths. We had a code word for that op. Only the men in the op knew it. That code word was in the subject line of each message.'

'And you can't trace the messages?'

'Sami tried. Someone doesn't want them to be traced and knows how to keep it that way.'

'And where does Sami come into all this? Was he in your unit, too?'

'He was the medical officer. If it wasn't for

his skill and care, I wouldn't be here now. He suffered great personal losses in the incident.'

Her mind moved on to a new horror. 'The interesting message you mentioned earlier. Did you mean it was *from* James or *about* James?' She paused as the unthinkable once again became thinkable. 'Did it say he was — ?' Fear brought her voice to a halt. Her throat worked as she fought to continue.

'No,' he said quickly, 'nothing like that. I'm fairly certain James sent it. The code word was in the subject line, like the other messages, but this message was one word, a word James would shout across a crowded bar to let me know something was wrong and I should watch my back. A private joke in a way.'

'So how did you answer it?'

'I said, 'E.N. phoned home.' ' The grin and dimple were back and a sparkle of good humor lit his eyes.

'E.N.,' she gasped. 'Did you receive a reply? Is that what Sami came in to tell you?'

The grin, dimple, and sparkle disappeared, leaving his face open for wariness. 'Yes, why? What's wrong?'

She took a deep, calming breath. 'It's just strange that you responded in that way because James calls me E.T. sometimes. My

48

middle name is Tally, my mother's maiden name.'

'I see. I don't want you to get your hopes up. His reply means nothing to Sami or to me.'

She jumped to her feet, her anticipation and dread spilling over. 'Just tell me what it said! If someone wants to kill James and you, then by coming here I'm standing in the same mess, as deeply as you are.'

'You're too quick.' He gave a resigned sigh. 'The message read, 'Noblesse oblige opens all doors.' '

She swayed, closing her eyes and saying a silent prayer of thanks. He was on his feet and steadying her in an instant.

'It's James. He's alive! Noblesse oblige is a play on my last name, part of the family joke I mentioned. I think he's acknowledging that I'm here, with you. The 'opens all doors' part might mean he'll come here, that we should expect him and leave the doors open.'

Impulsively, she flung her arms around Christovao Santos's neck in relief, and for support and comfort. At first, his muscles were hard and unyielding beneath the khaki material, and he held himself almost at attention. Then, just before she stepped away, he relaxed into her and put his big, warm hands on her back.

'Sorry,' she apologized in a small voice as she pulled away. '*Do* you think he'll come here?' She flicked away a stray tear.

He cleared his throat and gave a curt nod. 'We hope so. Sami sent a reply that James would understand, indicating that he should do so. Are you up to a little light exercise in the fresh air?' He offered her his arm. She took it without a second thought as reaction set in, leaving her exhausted and shaky.

Two sets of screened double doors opened from the *sala* onto a flagstone terrace at its back. A low, chest-high wall surrounded it, with beds of colorful blossoms and young trees standing out against the light stone. Healthy shrubs in huge hand-thrown pots occupied perfect spots on the flagstones. Off to one side sat a white wrought-iron table with a glass top. Matching chairs, cradling fat, floral-patterned cushions, clustered around it. A charming wooden gate opened into the outer compound where the outbuildings stood.

He appeared pleased with her delighted comments. 'I recently added this. My mother always wanted a terrace here. She designed it for me and,' he gestured toward the pots and the furniture, 'put things where they should be when it was finished.'

She smiled at his male view of the tricky

decorating and landscaping process. 'Your mother is a very talented lady. It's lovely, like a photograph out of a magazine.'

The night air was warm. The scent of green leaves and growing things from his fields, which surrounded the house, rode a gentle breeze. As they strolled around the terrace, he explained his home's layout to her.

His study, the library, and the combination *sala* and dining room were in the back section of the U-shaped house. As they faced the house from the terrace, the right wing housed the kitchen, at a right angle to the dining room area. Sami's suite, Mei's quarters, and storage areas were in that wing also. The left wing was devoted to the master bedroom and several guest rooms.

The largest room in the house, the *sala*, had four sets of screened double doors for ventilation, two onto the courtyard and two onto the terrace. Chris's study and the library each had two, one at the front and one at the back.

She appreciated his efforts to distract her, but James and the danger to him were foremost in her thoughts. 'Will you tell me about your 'accidents'?' she said into the companionable silence that had fallen between them.

Before he spoke, the muscle tensed in the

arm beneath her hand. 'At first it was vandalism aimed at Abundancia. Someone destroyed a newly planted field of coffee seedlings, then expensive farm machines were sabotaged, a whole equipment shed full of them. A big company is moving in around me. I thought they were just making their presence known.'

'But it turned out to be more personal?'

'I didn't think so at the time. Then it got nasty. I still run a few thousand head of cattle for meat for the workers and their families. Some were stolen, and some were deliberately maimed. I had to destroy about twenty head.'

She unclenched her jaws so she could speak. 'I hope there's a special place in hell for people who hurt animals.'

'I'm sure there is. Then it became really personal. Someone shot out my tires as I drove past a tall field, a field of corn almost ready for harvest. I lost control of the truck. It went into a ditch and rolled over several times. One of my foremen was with me. He broke his leg.'

'Well, that's certainly more obvious than the competition flexing its muscles. Subtle then escalating was the same pattern with James. But why put you two on your guard or make you angry?'

She felt his shrug. 'Maybe we're lucky, or

just harder to kill.'

She caught her breath and looked up at him out of the corner of her eye. 'Do you know who's doing this?'

'Maybe it's someone who has come back from the dead, and, no, I can't explain myself. I don't even know why I said it,' he added when she opened her mouth to speak. 'Somewhere between the cattle and the accident, I began getting the e-mails. I've doubled the guards on the roof since you arrived.'

She stopped walking, pulled her arm away from his, and studied the roofline of the *sala* wing. Several men patrolling the widow's walk were outlined against the starlit sky for a moment. Chris turned to her, anticipating her response.

'So that's what that is!' She paused as the implications became clear. 'I didn't surprise you that night,' she said in an accusing voice. 'This place is a mini-fortress. You knew I was there, in your study, didn't you?'

# 4

Chris made a typically Latin male gesture, shrugging with both hands at hip level and presented palms up. 'We're isolated here. When I took over Abundancia, I put some things into place in case I ever had to defend or protect my home. Once a soldier, always a soldier. And I assure you the house has been a mini-fortress for only a short time, since my accident. We usually don't live and work under armed guard like this.'

She had given up trying to understand men's fascination with playing soldiers, although she'd been surrounded by military men all her life. She and her mother had decided long ago that it must be in their hard wiring.

'So why didn't the guards stop me?'

'I knew you were on my land from the moment you crossed the perimeter we had set up. The guards have orders to report any intruders to me, but not to interfere, unless they see weapons. They alerted me about a lone, bedraggled woman who was falling over her own feet. The roof guards verified you'd gone where we wanted you to go. None of us thought you had a gun. Where did you get it, by the way?'

'I found it in the glove box of my rental car. Is it standard equipment here? I brought it along to make you take me seriously.' She smiled ruefully. 'By the time I got here, the fever had a firm grip and I didn't feel very convincing.'

His next words sobered her. 'That gun and the fact that you fired it almost got you killed. According to our plan, Sami was in place before I went into my study. Everything Sami does with his hands, he does efficiently. That includes killing, if the situation calls for it.'

'But where . . . ? There was a wall behind me. I made sure of that before you came into the room . . . Oh. A secret panel?'

He smiled appreciatively. 'With a couple of days' worth of sleep and some food in you, you're quick. Not well-dressed, but quick. Yes, there's a well-oiled hidden door between my study and the library.'

'I think I hate you, Christovao Santos. And the next time I see Sami, I'll thank him for using restraint.' She sighed and plopped down in the nearest patio chair to rest.

He took the hint and joined her. 'I'm tiring you. I'll carry you back to your room, if you like.'

She would like. Very much. Now, where

had that come from? *Emily Tally Noble, you will not fall 'in like' with this military man. Not even 'in interest' with him.*

She stared at him while her mouth opened and closed. 'N-no. Thanks. Just let me regroup. I'll be fine in a few minutes.'

'Who taught you about guns? Your father? James?'

'James. And he taught me some basic self-defense. I had some strange talents for a girl because of James. He made me play soldier with him from about age four, and I was very good at all his video war games and the arcade games. I'm still pretty good at them. I occasionally pop into an arcade just to weird out the regulars. With my father working most of his life on military bases in the United Kingdom, James was in heaven.

'But enough about me. Tell me about this beautiful place. What do you grow at Abundancia?'

He was obviously pleased by her interest. 'Thanks to my father, the fields closest to the house, the fields you saw on your way here, are old cultivated land. I rotate crops of rice, edible beans, corn, more edible beans, soybeans, and cotton in them. Other sections are in coffee, bananas, papayas, and other fruits. Besides cotton, those are the high-value crops. We have a continuous planting rotation that is seldom delayed by weather. If we have a *vecancio*, a mini-drought, we use wells to irrigate. So far, well drilling isn't regulated in the *cerrados*.'

'I'd love a guided tour sometime. With the fever and the constant worry about James, I don't remember much of what I saw the day I drove down. I'm not even sure how I got here in one piece. Has James ever been here?'

'Oh, many times. Every time his work brings him to South America, he visits or I meet him in Rio.'

'Ah, yes, the women-chasing adventures you mentioned earlier. I notice the land is very flat. Does that mean we'll see them coming, whoever *they* are?'

He ignored her question. 'Flat as a tabletop. The *cerrados* is Brazil's tropical high plains. We have endless vistas here. The plains are sometimes broken by small rivers that have carved out wide valleys.'

'Sounds lovely. *Cerrados*. I love to say it, but what does it mean?' The word sounded especially nice when he said it, rolling the 'r' sounds.

'It translates from the Portuguese as 'closed, inaccessible wasteland.' That's exactly what it was until Brasilia was built in the 1960s. The *cerrados* was isolated by lack of roads or any other access before that.

Extensive livestock operations finally opened it up.'

As much as she hated to admit it to herself, she found Christovao Santos and his life here fascinating and wanted to know everything about both. 'Has Abundancia always been your home?'

'Yes, I was born here. My father came here originally to help develop a 'tropical' soybean and the techniques for managing the *cerrados* soils.'

'Managing? What's wrong with them? It's so lush all around.'

'Only because we have made it yield. *Cerrados* soils are ancient and have low fertility. They are, however, deep and permeable. They require extensive fertilization and chemical correction before crops will grow. It takes several crop years to achieve fertile soil on newly opened land.'

One detail she remembered about her drive, before things got fuzzy, was that the fields were extensive, going on as far as the eye could see. If there hadn't been signs along the dirt roads that ran between them, directing her to *Casa Abundancia,* she never would have found the house among the vast fields.

'How many acres do you farm?'

'In Brazil we use hectares. Most *cerrados*

farms run to two thousand hectares and some to ten thousand. I own fifteen thousand hectares. That translates to thirty-seven thousand, five hundred acres. But less than two-thirds of that is under cultivation. The remainder is under the soil amendment process.'

She stared in shock. 'You own enough land to be your own small country.'

It must have taken his father's lifetime to clear land and correct the soil for cultivation, and now it would take Chris's to finish the job.

'It seems strange that an ex-mercenary should become a farmer and offer farming jobs to other ex-soldiers, but apparently I'm surrounded by living examples. I've read that growing and cultivating plants is healing.'

'It is. Actually, it was the other way around. I was a farmer then a soldier who became a mercenary. After I reexamined my life, I became a farmer again.'

She hesitated, studying the man beside her. 'May I ask you a personal question?'

'I'm sure you will, regardless of what I say, but I appreciate your warning me.' He looked wary, despite his smile.

'You don't sound Brazilian. Not all the time, anyway. Have you spent time in the States?'

'I'm a hybrid, too, and I also hold dual citizenship. My mother is an American. My father went to the States to encourage American farm machinery manufacturers to come to the *cerrados*. Her father, my grandfather, was in that business. That's how they met. My mother made sure I was bilingual, and she took me to visit relatives in the U.S. every year. She lives there now, in the South. She visits Abundancia several times a year. Any decorating or style in the house is due to her, except your — except the room you're in.'

Well, that answered one of her questions. The mystery woman must have been a live-in girlfriend. 'Your mother sounds wonderful. I'd love to meet her sometime. So, will it be possible for me to see any of your farming operation while I'm here?'

'Distances are vast in the *cerrados*. Abundancia itself is vast. I'll show you around the local portion once things are back to normal, or as soon as your bruises heal, perhaps?' He grinned. 'Under the present circumstances, we couldn't venture far and we wouldn't go alone.'

She grinned back. 'Definitely after they fade. But my bruises will have to take care of themselves for a while, I'm afraid, because I have to go shopping. Now. I need clothes,

Chris, especially more underwear. If you insist that I stay here for my safety then I'd like to wear my own clothes rather than yours. And I need girl stuff.'

'Oh. I didn't think of that.'

'Could we at least check to see if the airline found my bag? I asked them to send it to a hotel in Barreiras.'

He hesitated, frowning. 'That's not a good idea. We could take some men and go to Barreiras tomorrow, if you're up to it, to get whatever you need. Being a woman and curious as Gato, you probably looked inside the closet in your room. Choose something from it to wear tomorrow, including a hat to hide your hair.'

'Oh, I see. I'm going undercover.'

'No, *I'm* going under duress.'

She couldn't stop her smile. 'Well, I appreciate your efforts on my behalf. And I won't ask about the clothes. I wonder, though, why you put me in that bedroom when you have others to choose from.'

'I didn't put you in it.' He frowned heavily. 'Sami did.'

'Sami? Why would he do that?'

Exasperation was plain in his voice. 'You're as relentless and wearing as water dripping on stone. Do you know that?'

'I believe it has come up in conversation

61

before. And why did Sami pick that room?'

'Because he's taken leave of his senses. He tells me you're the one who will change my mind about certain decisions I made after a broken relationship.'

'Oh, the marriage and children thing?' Then a totally new interpretation of 'decisions' flopped into place. She spoke aloud, out of astonishment, before she thought through her words. 'You'll never make me believe you're gay and those clothes are yours.'

He stared at her, his mouth hanging open until he closed it with a snap. 'I'm sure I can convince you, without a doubt, that I'm not gay. Shall I prove it?' he asked.

She held up a restraining hand, erupting into gales of laughter before she could speak. 'I'm sorry,' she managed. 'No woman worth her mascara would make that mistake about you. I'll blame it on my being ill. And I did say I'd never believe it.'

When she had herself under control, she asked, 'Did Sami say why he believes that? Other than taking leave of his senses, that is.'

For several moments he gave a great impression of a man sitting in an uncomfortable chair. 'I think it's because you shot at me. There's only one other woman I know who would have pulled that trigger.'

She figured it out instantly. 'Your mother.'

His eyes narrowed as he studied her. 'Yes. Now, I really don't wish to discuss this any further.'

'Fine. Just let me assure you that I don't want to change your mind about anything, except my car keys and my passport. And I could ask Mei if she has something I can wear tomorrow if you'd rather I didn't . . . ' The look on his face made her voice trail off. 'Okay, I'll do as you say,' she added quickly.

Their problem suddenly seemed like safer ground. 'Will you answer a question about our situation here? You suspect the common thread is the mercenary operation gone bad. If you or James or Sami aren't behind it, all survivors, then who can it be? How many survivors did you say are left?'

'I didn't.' He stood up and indicated they should go back to the *sala*. 'You don't give up easily, do you? I've already compromised your safety by telling you more than you need to know. I won't even touch on how much you've pried out of me this evening about my personal life.'

This time she slipped her arm through his without his offering it, simply because it felt like it belonged there. 'Oh, your secrets are safe with me. And I compromised my own safety when I barged into your house. Just tell me what I'm supposed to do if someone starts shooting. How do I know which are our guys and which are the enemy? Whom should I run to?'

'Don't do anything, especially run. If someone starts shooting, just hit the dirt and stay there. Someone will come to you.'

Her eyes widened and she looked up at him. 'That's not very reassuring, since the enemy would come to me, too, to murder me. It looks like that's the point of the exercise, doesn't it? No survivors, even someone like me who just happens to stumble in and get in the way.'

He jerked to a halt, and his right arm convulsed, squeezing her arm against his side. In the light from the *sala* doorway, she watched him pale beneath his tan skin tone. Swinging around, he blocked her path with his broad-shouldered body. His voice was level, but held the heat of a blowtorch just the same.

'*Jesus Doce!* So many questions. It was not meant to be reassuring. It's what I'm ordering you to do if something happens. You *will* do it. *Compreendo?*' His stance, legs apart and braced, fists clenched, shoulders taut, verified for her that he had been a fighting man. His tone left her in no doubt that he had been an officer.

She backpedaled, trying to reassure her brother's touchy friend. 'I'm not a fool, *senhor*. I'll do as you say.'

Gato had kept pace with them. Now, he stopped and sat down, looking from one to the other as each spoke.

'Good.' Chris appeared somewhat mollified.

Unfortunately, she didn't stop there. 'When James shows up, couldn't he come home with me until you find out what's going on?'

He muttered and closed his eyes. She was sure he was counting to ten. Or praying. In Portuguese. 'You either have great confidence in my training and abilities, or you think I'm totally expendable. I won't ask which. I need and want James's help, if he's able. Besides, you would never make it out of Brazil alive. Someone would surely kill you just to stop the noise.' His voice rose slightly on the last words.

Her laugh started as a giggle then grew. She watched his handsome face reflect shock then exasperation then guarded amusement.

'I'm sorry, Chris. I apologize for my chatter. I do that when I'm nervous. Sarcasm is another service I offer when I'm scared. I'm both right now, so you're getting both barrels.'

He took her by the shoulders and gave her

one gentle shake. 'I'm glad you're scared. Stay that way, because the man who might be behind these incidents and deaths is utterly ruthless. He'd use you without a second thought to get to James and to me. That's why you have to do what I tell you, when I tell you, without hesitation.' His eyes narrowed. 'What is it?'

She'd gone very still at his words, because they brought to the surface of her sluggish brain what she couldn't remember earlier. One of the men in James's flat had asked her about some papers they thought James had. And they had meant to take her with them, to kidnap her. These were memories she'd rather share when James was safe with her.

'Nothing's wrong. I think all this is starting to hit me.'

He was quick. 'You should tell me anything you remember, you know. It might be important.'

'I-I didn't remember anything.'

His hands dropped away and his features turned wooden. 'I think you'd better go to bed before I shoot you myself.'

He held himself so stiff and straight that she was sure she could lean him back on his heels against a wall for storage. Christovao Santos had a lot of emotional baggage, no doubt about it. The mystery woman and the bad op had both done real numbers on him and his personality.

She smiled in the face of his dismissal. 'What, no chess game?'

He used his accent-heavy formal voice. 'What you've told me and your presence here have brought home the gravity of the situation. I must take additional steps to ensure the safety of Abundancia, you, and my workers. And now I have preparations to make for a trip to Barreiras tomorrow. Please let me make them, Emily Noble. *Boa noite*.'

He didn't move. She apparently was not going into the *sala* again that night. Gato meowed softly to reinforce the order.

'I'm coming,' she said to the cat. 'If Gato is bunking with me, may I have his brush and some toys, please?'

'I'll send them with Luiz.' He now stood at ease, hands behind his back.

'Well then. *Muito obrigado* and *boa noite*.'

He winced. 'Your accent is — interesting.'

'I know. I'll work on it while I'm here. I have no aptitude for speaking other languages, but I have the constitution of a horse. My mother said it was one of life's trade-offs. I bounce back quickly from illness and injury.'

'I've noticed. Your vocal abilities appear especially resilient. Good night.'

The length of tile walk to her door was unnaturally long with his gaze boring into her back the whole way. She concentrated on forgetting the long list of nasty things that had happened to her recently by focusing on her short to-do list, like finding an outfit to wear out in public tomorrow. She admitted the truth to herself. She couldn't wait to get her hands on the clothes she'd glimpsed in that closet. And she even had Chris's permission to explore.

She flung open the louvered closet doors the moment the room door closed behind her. Gato settled on the bed to watch, adopting a sphinx pose with his front legs stretched out in front of him. The labels in the garments all read the same, Maria of Rio, and the rich materials and diverse textures felt alive beneath her fingers as she brushed them along the long, luxurious row. Brights and pastel colors floated before her eyes, reminding her of meadows of wildflowers. And in contrast to the rainbow hues, her favorite color stood out among them. There was nothing like sleek, elegant, classic black to make a girl feel special.

She was in the midst of a trying on orgy when a knock sounded at her door. She looked down over the daring, shimmering black sheath cocktail dress she wore at that moment. It sparkled in the light and the turned-up, lettuce-leaf edge of the slightly flaring skirt moved like a living thing with every step. It was made to dance in. She couldn't get out of the luscious confection quickly, nor did she want to. So, she wagered with herself that Chris had sent Luiz with Gato's things, as he had said he would, and it was not her prickly host on the other side of door number one.

She lost the wager rather spectacularly. Christovao Santos stood on her doorstep, nearly filling the opening. In one white-knuckled fist he clutched a brush and a catnip ball that squeaked when his fingers involuntarily tightened around it. A laser mouse pointer toy on a key ring dangled from the thumb of his other fist. He sucked in his breath when he first saw her, his eyes glittering like dewdrops on violets in the light that poured out into the night from behind her.

Emily had reached two conclusions approximately half an hour before Chris's unexpected appearance. The first was that the mystery woman had impeccable taste in clothes. The second was that Maria of Rio was a genius. She also had figured out a few details about the mystery woman's physical appearance from the clothes themselves. She was several inches shorter than Emily's own five feet seven inches, her bust was slightly smaller, and she had rather large feet for her size. But the shoes that matched the dress fit, though they were a little tight.

What Emily unexpectedly realized now, with Christovao Santos's intense gaze sweeping over her, was that these physical differences resulted in the dress being shorter on her, well above her knees, than it would have been on its owner. And her cleavage, while not eye-popping, was considerable. Her fading bruises ruined the whole outfit, in her opinion.

Christovao Santos seemingly took in these startling adaptations to his beloved's dress, and much more, in a long, silent, hot, comprehensive stare. When he opened his mouth, to speak or to snarl, she decided that humble apologies, launched into immediately, would be a good move on her part.

'I'm so sorry, Chris. I was hoping it wasn't you at the door,' she blurted, feeling her cheeks grow warm when she realized her admission. 'No! I mean I couldn't resist trying on this dress. She has great taste in clothes, whoever she is, and we're almost the same size.'

When he still did not or could not speak, yet his mouth remained open, she heard her nervous voice fill the vacuum. 'You're struck dumb by my audacity, no doubt. Well, so am I, now that I stop to think about it. I'm so very sorry. It's just that the clothes are so lovely. Look, why don't I remove myself from temptation into another room? I have nothing to move, really, so it will only take a minute. Just let me grab some slacks and a top for tomorrow and I'll — '

She backed away when he took one long stride into the room and slammed the door behind him. She briefly met the astonished, appreciative stare of a man, smiling and wearing camouflage, who stood on the tile walk behind and to the right of Christovao Santos. The automatic weapon slung over his shoulder glinted briefly before the door closed between them, although he leaned far to his right to keep her in sight as long as possible. She snapped upright from her own leftward lean, once the disappearing man . . . disappeared.

'I-I'm sincerely sorry,' she repeated, continuing her slow, backward journey across the room. 'I've abused your hospitality tonight, the hospitality you so kindly extended after I shot at you and everything. And now you find me wearing a dress owned by the woman you — '

She broke off when he looked past her to

the bed. Considering what had happened to her last time, she thought it wise to follow his gaze this go-round. She saw what he saw, heaps of women's clothing strewn over the bed's surface. Gato peered out at them from beneath a froth of ivory lace, looking like the resident party animal caught enjoying a decadent night on the town.

'Correction. You find me going through her clothes like you're having a yard sale or something,' she admitted quietly then gulped. 'If it's any consolation, James will kill me when he finds out what I've done.'

He stopped advancing, roughly eighteen inches from where she had run aground against one of the posters at the foot of the bed. 'I just might save James the trouble,' he said in a choked voice.

She put her hands behind her back and ducked her head, awaiting the angry words he would, with just cause, heap upon her. When they didn't come, she looked up.

The movement caused the comb holding her hair to finally give up its tenuous grip. She'd used it, after she found it in a drawer, to try a hasty, experimental, upswept hairstyle to go with the dress. She reached up and yanked it out, letting the tumbled white-gold mass settle around her mostly bare shoulders.

His eyes narrowed to violet slits, while his

breath escaped in a hiss. He cleared his throat before he spoke again, in a tight voice. 'I brought you these.'

He shoved Gato's possessions at her. The ring part of the laser mouse toy was stuck on his thumb and they had a time-out while she removed it for him, with some difficulty.

'I also came to apologize for losing my temper earlier and for swearing at you,' he continued when he was free.

'*Jesus Doce?* Does it mean Sweet — ?' She caught his look and reconsidered the question. 'I mean, thank you for apologizing, but it's not necessary. People swear at me all the time, actually.'

'I don't doubt that for a moment,' he said. 'I also came to tell you that I've put a guard on your door and one outside the bathroom window at the back. I don't want to move you because this room is close to mine, in case something happens.'

He turned and walked to the door, pausing with his hand on the knob. 'I've never seen that dress before tonight. You may have it, if you like.' He hesitated. 'It suits you. She is dark, where you are fair. I've always thought that blondes hold the advantage in black.'

Then he was gone.

# 5

She sorted through Christovao Santos's words, grateful that they had been mild and few in number, considering her offense. Her mind latched on to the four that would give her nightmares, 'in case something happens.' Moving like a centipede on a stimulant, she locked the door, peeled off the dress, shrugged on her T-shirt, then hung everything neatly back in the closet, including the black dress. It pained her to think of all those lovely things shut away from the light that gave them life.

After that, she unearthed a pair of dressy slacks, a silk blouse, a hat, decent shoes, and a large purse for the next day's journey. She was in bed within half an hour. Eventually, she slept.

Much too early the next morning, someone tapped on her door. She snapped awake at the sound.

'Déjà vu all over again,' she muttered, staggering out of the heavenly bed.

Her lessons, though usually painful, were well and speedily learned. Things that had happened in her life and certain aspects of

74

her personality necessitated her being a quick study. So, she unlocked the door — and cautiously opened it a mere crack. What she saw on her doorstep made her step back in surprise, opening the door wider at the same time.

A tiny Oriental dynamo blew through the opening into the room, bringing the bright morning along for the ride. The woman crossed to the bed, set down the breakfast tray she carried, and turned to face Emily, folding her hands demurely.

Emily closed the door on the new grinning, staring guard, who had gaped his fill of her in Chris's T-shirt, and squinted at her visitor. 'You must be Mei. Do you speak English?'

'English, yes. A little. Portuguese, yes. A little.'

The woman, at attention, could stand under Emily's arm, yet she carried herself like a bird colonel. Emily smiled at this observation then rubbed her eyes sleepily.

'Thank you for helping me to undress, and for anything else you did for me when I was ill, Mei. I'm glad there's another woman around the place.'

Mei did a little half bow, showing the bun of graying hair pinned to the top of her head, and then nodded. 'No woman in house but me. 'Til now. *Patrao* no allow.'

That admission woke her fully. 'Do you mean Senhor Santos doesn't allow women, any women, at Abundancia?'

Mei nodded vigorously. 'You eat. *Patrao* says you come after you eat. He no like wait.'

Emily stood rooted to the spot. That mysterious dark-haired woman who was shorter than she was, and who had great taste in clothes and the money to indulge it, had crashed and burned the *patrao* big time. Unless —

A new thought, a possible new meaning to all this, flooded through her. 'Oh, heavens, is she dead? Mei, the woman who stayed in this room, is she dead?'

Mei shook her head solemnly. 'No dead. *Fugir*. Run away.' Her tiny mouth drew into a straight, stubborn line and she marched to the door, making her escape while Emily absorbed that parting shot. She glanced at the full closet and gave a long, low whistle.

Then she pictured the tough, angry ex-soldier, ex-mercenary, who had been in this room with her last night. Would *she* hang around to pack the goodies if she meant to leave him? Hell, no. Much wiser to take what's on your back and what you can stuff into your pockets and purse and — *fugir*. Emily decided that a nice long girl talk with Mei in the kitchen was called for, as soon as

76

she could work it in.

Vehicle engines thrummed somewhere outside the wood gate as she crossed the courtyard diagonally to the *sala*. Chris waited for her inside.

He pulled a bush hat with a leather hatband low over his eyes when he saw her. '*Bom dia*, Emily Noble. Did you sleep well?'

'No. I just couldn't summon up any warm, cozy, protected feelings generated by large men carrying big guns outside my room.'

'You will,' he said simply, taking her arm, 'once you have the need of large men carrying big guns.'

He ushered her out the *sala* doors on the other side of the room, onto the terrace, through the squeaky terrace gate, and into the outer compound.

'We have a long drive ahead of us. Where's your hat?'

Reaching into the oversize woven purse hanging on her shoulder, she pulled out a pair of sunglasses and a crushable sun hat. She bracketed the large glasses over her eyes, covering half her face. Bending from the waist, she filled the hat's crown with her hair. When she stood upright, she seated it on her head and adjusted the brim at a rakish angle. '*Bom, senhor?*'

'*Bom, senhorita.*' He had slipped on aviator

sunglasses, so she couldn't read his eyes, but he stood very still for several seconds, looking down at her, much longer than it would take to evaluate her disguise. Finally, he took her arm again and urged her forward. 'You'll pay cash today.'

She pulled back. 'Oh, wait. I don't have much cash. I thought I'd — '

'Don't start thinking this early in the day. My nerves won't stand it.' He tugged her forward. 'I'll pay. No traveler's checks or credit card, either. You'll leave no paper trail, other than the broad, littered one you've already left in your wake. *Compreendo?* I don't have many illusions about nobody knowing your whereabouts, but I cling to those few desperately. And don't take off your hat or sunglasses.'

She skipped to keep up with his stride. 'I'll pay you back. In fact, I'll make James pay you back because my being here is his fault anyway. But how can I look at or try on clothes with sunglasses and a hat on?'

'You won't. Just grab jeans and T-shirts and . . . things . . . in your size.' He totally ignored the look of disbelief she threw his way. 'I won't dress for dinner and make you feel inferior while you're here. How's that?'

He opened the door of a Land Rover for her to climb inside then went to talk to his men. She used the time to look around her. In front of their vehicle sat a pickup truck. Close behind their vehicle sat another pickup truck. Two men with watchful eyes waited in each, all of them smoking pungent, ugly, brown cigarettes, a cheaper brand than the cigarillos Chris smoked. Two more men waited to open and close the large wooden gates that opened out of the outer compound. All the vehicles were older models but their engines hummed in a well-tuned trio. Chris finally climbed in beside her.

'How much heat ya packin', han'some?' she drawled in her best Mae West imitation.

He didn't even glance at her while he fastened his seat belt. 'Enough.'

'A man and his gun. It's a beautiful thing.'

She sat quietly for a few minutes, taking in the vastness of his tall fields, because as soon as the outer gates closed behind them, they were among them.

'I hope I can translate my sizes into Portuguese. I remember what the tags read, um, last night.' Her gaze slid his way to see if he reacted to her mention of last night's fiasco.

'You'll be fine then,' he said, eyes straight ahead.

They soon passed a row of what looked like short silos housed under one roof. She shivered and felt the hairs on the back of her neck stand upright on their roots. 'What are those? There are so many places to . . . ' Her voice died away.

He glanced at her then. 'So many places to hide?'

She nodded. 'These tall fields are like a jungle or a maze. You could hide an army in one of them.'

'We're taking a calculated risk here. Nothing more. Try not to worry. My men did a sweep of the area before we left the house.'

'How do you sweep a cornfield? It sounds like a bad joke.'

'Just don't go into one unless you plan to be there for a while. Each year several children and occasionally a worker will get lost in them.'

When she didn't answer immediately, he continued, 'Those were the northern silos for grain storage back there. Abundancia cleans and bags its rice and edible beans. It adds value to them when they're hauled to the buying stations. We mill it for some neighboring farms as well.'

She was grateful to him for trying to take her mind off this feeling of exposure, of being watched. So, she took a good look at another group of buildings they were passing through and continued to ask questions.

'Who hauls them for you?'

'Several of the larger operations, including mine, formed a co-op fleet of trucks. They go from farm to farm and pick up the harvest or the bagged grain.'

'And these long sheds? Ah, machinery. The northern equipment sheds?'

'Correct. Abundancia has lots and lots of machine sheds and shops. I keep several crews of mechanics to maintain and service our equipment. During planting and harvest, our tractors run day and night. They must be repaired and back in service immediately, if they break down. They often do when we put thousands of hours a year on most of them.'

The flat fields of lush plants of varying heights and colors rolled away as far as the eye could see, surrounding them. 'This reminds me of the grain belts in the U.S. and Canada.'

'They're very like one another. The *cerrados* is about the size of the U.S. east of the Mississippi. It covers one-fourth of Brazil, most of it south of the equator.'

'Are the farms owned by families or companies?'

'Most are family farms and the families live on them. Those with school-age children sometimes live in Barreiras or Luis Eduardo

81

Magalhaes part of the time to be close to the schools.'

'If I lived here, I'd home school my kids for as long as I possibly could.'

His voice changed, becoming more cautious. 'It's a lonely life for a woman in the *cerrados*.'

'For some women I'm sure it is.'

He glanced at her and made a little sound. 'But not you, right? You're different?' The words dripped sarcasm.

'I'm self-contained. Hypothetically speaking, if I lived in the *cerrados* I'd still have my work, those hypothetical children to educate and love, hypothetical meals to prepare because I'd want to do most of the cooking, and I'd have a hypothetical husband to keep happy.'

She heard a smile in his voice now. 'And you'd probably organize the other wives to revolt.'

'Hmmm. I'd probably organize dances, play groups, continuing education classes, and a craft club or a book club. Hypothetically.' She felt his stare briefly on her profile until she pointed out to him that the pickup ahead of them had just swerved to avoid a huge pothole with a tree branch stuck upright in it.

They traveled a great distance in silence,

until she pulled her attention away from the pretty fields. 'How far is Barreiras? It felt like I drove forever to get to Abundancia.'

'The farmstead is ninety kilometers from Barreiras and most of my land spreads out south from the house. My father bought up land then cleared it and expanded south in a circular pattern, as I must do in some areas, mimicking the irrigation pivots we have to use in times of drought.'

'The wells you mentioned?'

'Yes. One well pumping into a central reservoir can irrigate three one hundred-hectare pivots. We run the pumps from eleven p.m. until seven a.m., when the electrical rates are lower. I'll have to use them if we don't get rain soon.'

'And where do your workers live?'

'I provide small houses for families and dormitories for the unmarried men. The land to the south is dotted with many equipment sheds, grain storage silos, and housing and dining facilities for the workers, most of whom are former soldiers, as I explained last night. All the facilities here have electricity, which isn't the case on some farms.'

She nodded her approval. 'You sound like a caring, compassionate employer, Chris.'

She'd driven the roads to Abundancia in

a daze of exhaustion and fever. Now, wide-awake and well, she saw why, besides her physical condition, it had taken her so long to drive the ninety kilometers from Barreiras. Some of the dirt roads on and around the farm were bumpy and uneven, while the two-lane paved roads were riddled with potholes, the deeper ones marked with tree branches to get the driver's attention.

At the airport in Barreiras, a group of American students had taken her aside from the rental car desk and educated her about Brazilian roads. And the roads had lived down to the entire list of things they had warned her about. No interstate highway, as she recognized it, existed in Brazil. Dirt roads were the rule in remote areas, and those quickly became impassable when it rained. Road maintenance was spotty, and roadside assistance was nonexistent.

As she told him about her road trip, his laughter punctuated her words. 'I learned the rest the hard way, when I drove through Barreiras then south to you. Heavy truck traffic rules. Traffic laws aren't enforced. Rules of the road are looked upon as suggestions. Stop signs are treated as yield signs. Among the trucks, I encountered pedestrians of all descriptions, bicycles of all descriptions, and one horse-drawn wagon that defied description. It was like driving in an arcade game.'

She was tired after that, and they fell into a companionable silence. The radio crackled periodically as the other drivers checked in. She slept for the rest of the journey, but Chris woke her in good time to see the approach to Barreiras.

She'd been surprised at the size of Barreiras when her plane landed there and when she drove out of the city in her rented car. She was more impressed now, a week later, when she was able to concentrate on what the city had to offer. She asked Chris about this main city of Western Bahia.

'Around one hundred thirty thousand people live here. Luis Eduardo Magalhaes, about ninety kilometers west, has a population of around twenty thousand. We have everything you might want. Both towns have schools, banks, hospitals and clinics, shops, restaurants, hotels, besides machinery, fertilizer and chemical dealers, and TV and radio stations.'

When they had reached the outskirts of the city, the pickup trucks blended into the traffic around them, pulling over, turning occasionally, or passing them at other times. She made a game of trying to keep up with their maneuvers, finally giving up in confusion and frustration.

Downtown Barreiras bustled with people and activity. Chris pointed out several supermarkets and a large farmer's market that was open daily except Sunday. She saw hundreds of stores, appliance stores, furniture stores, satellite TV stores, cellular phone stores, and more clothing stores than she ever dreamed might be located in the middle of Brazil.

She felt afraid suddenly and didn't know why. Her breath came fast and shallow. 'Don't ask me to pick one, Chris, because I can't. I feel totally overwhelmed.'

He shot her a look and, then much to her surprise, he swung the Land Rover into a parking space in front of one of the upscale department stores, one whose name she recognized.

'Designer jeans?' she gasped. 'I wonder if James can afford them.'

'I don't care whose name is on your . . . on them, just so you can move in them.'

She turned on the seat to face him, taking a deep, calming breath. 'And hit the dirt in them. Let's not forget that. Are you coming in with me?'

He checked all the mirrors for their pickup pals. 'Of course. You go nowhere alone. Nowhere, remember that.'

'Yes, sir.' His look stopped the movement of her hand when it was halfway to her brow in a salute. 'I have to visit the drugstore next door first. Every girl needs chocolate, lipstick, and a decent moisturizer, you know. I only have sample sizes in my carry-on.'

Inside the store, she pulled her sunglasses down on her nose and looked over the top to do her shopping. Fascinated, she studied Chris as much as she looked at the shelves. His eyes never stopped moving, sweeping the other customers, the doors, the front windows, even the floor and ceiling. The first time he looked upward, she looked up, too. He frowned at her, before he smiled and gave a tiny shake of his head. She looked away and tried not to watch him after that.

He managed to pick up a tablet of old-fashioned shaving soap and carry it to the checkout with her.

'Let me guess,' she whispered as she took cosmetics, personal items, deodorant, shampoo, toothpaste, bubble bath, a candle for the edge of the bathtub, and M&Ms, among other things, out of her basket. 'You use a straight razor. Doubles as a weapon?'

He hissed a phrase in Portuguese. She interpreted it to mean 'Shut up,' so she did.

They locked their purchases in the Land Rover. She spied one of the pickup trucks parked a few spaces behind them. The other one passed on the street before she turned to go into the department store. One man sat in each truck now.

'Stop looking at our men,' Chris said softly, bending close to her so he could whisper in her ear. 'It draws attention to them and possible fire to us. That irritates everyone around you. Like me.'

The sleek, doe-eyed female sales clerks instantly recognized Christovao Santos and clustered around him. She stood aside, a little smile on her face, and watched the man work the adoring throng. He spoke. The clerks listened then scattered, eager to please him. The *patrao* might not allow women at Abundancia but she'd bet he got all the action he could handle when he cut loose in Barreiras, Brasilia, or Rio.

'I explained to them that you want basics. And shoes.' He never once met her eyes while he spoke to her. Instead, he scanned the area 180 degrees around them.

That broke her semblance of calm. 'Will you stop doing that! You're making me so nervous I can't think.' Her voice was sharper than she intended, but it worked. His gaze finally came to rest on her glare, aimed at him over the top of her sunglasses. She had no doubt that he saw fear written there, too, because that's what she felt.

He did his male Latin shrug. 'This is how I react to the hunt. My training kicks in. Never allow yourself to feel like the hunted. Always be the hunter. Take the initiative.'

'The hunt? The hunter?' A definite squeak hung off the ends of the words. 'It's like a foreign language to me.'

He frowned, his voice sharper than hers had been. 'On the offensive then. Security is really not your problem, Emily. Buy your things and let's get out of here.'

'You're right. Security is *your* problem. Finding James is *my* problem.' She stomped over to a rack of jeans where a clerk waited with a tape measure.

The various clerks fell over themselves trying to help her and, thereby, impress Chris. In a few minutes, she had a stack of jeans, shorts, T-shirts, crop tops, three embroidered shirts, two plain skirts, and a cardigan sweater. A lively little discussion ensued when, over Chris's protests, she insisted she would try on one of each of those items before she left the store. She won by pointing out that the clothes would do her no good if she got them home and found they didn't fit.

'Every five minutes,' he muttered, 'open that door and pretend to show me something, or I'll break the damned door down.'

'Okay,' she whispered back, 'every five minutes I'll flash you.'

As for underwear, bras, and socks, she relied on the measurements a clerk had taken, plus the woman's suggestions about sizing. They had piled all the items near the cash register. She tried on a pair of sandals, some slippers, and a pair of running shoes and added them to the heap on the counter. Two embroidered white eyelet cotton nightgowns and a matching duster joined the stack.

She gathered up the items she wanted to try on, and yet another clerk showed her to a large, elegantly decorated fitting room. She last glimpsed Chris, frowning and with eyes glinting, as he took up a casually on-guard pose at the entrance to the fitting room area.

It felt good to be rid of the stupid hat and sunglasses . . . and the tension, if only for a little while. She was beginning to feel the few more thousand miles of worry and fear she had on her. She took several relaxing breaths before she shook out her hair, stripped down to her bra and panties, and shrugged on the embroidered cotton shirt she'd chosen to try on. It was a slightly oversized, comfortable fit, covering her to just below the tops of her thighs. Her fingers sought the cotton material, soft to the touch and light enough to breathe. The embroidery was exquisite —

Behind her a large, dark object dropped from the ceiling into the fitting room with barely a thud. She stared, dumb-founded, into the mirror. Now she understood Chris's need to look upward in his constant room scans. A rangy, rough-looking peasant or laborer or whatever the hell they were called here, tall and scowling, stared back at her.

Oh, God, she was going to die or be kidnapped in a fitting room in Brazil! Any second now, as soon as she got over the shock, she would scream or do something useful. Why should this bastard have it all his own way? Chris wasn't far away. And it helped to remember how she'd used her initiative, Chris's word, to escape the men in London.

She refused to die here. She simply would not. And because here stood yet another obstacle in her path to finding James, she let anger carry her along. She wouldn't give in without a fight. She was just in the mood.

She swung around to face her attacker . . . then he smiled.

'So, what the bloody hell are you doing in Brazil, E.T.?' her brother's familiar, beloved voice said in a harsh whisper.

'J-James? Oh, thank God!' She flung herself at him, gave him a quick hug, then stepped back, hands on hips. 'James! I thought you were dead or hurt or — Of course, I also thought you were an ordinary Royal Engineer, but you were a mercenary?'

'Only for one op!' He looked awful, even in the complimentary lighting of the room.

'One was enough, apparently. How could you keep a bombshell like that from me?'

He held up a hand to stop her flow of words. 'Nice seeing you, too, Em. Call Chris in — '

'Don't call me Em!' That hated childhood nickname he'd teased her with still grated on her nerves like finger-nails on a chalkboard.

'Sorry. Emily. Call Chris in. I need some help, and we have to find out how he wants to handle this. You've put yourself in danger by coming here, you know. Why didn't you stay — ?' He peered at her more closely, noting her bruised face. 'What's happened to you?'

'*I'm* in danger? According to Rent-A-Revolt out there, the survivors of his old unit are being picked off like Chippendale dancers at a bachelor auction,' she hissed. 'Are you sure we can trust him?'

His shocked face took on a look she knew well. 'Listen to me or I'll sock you,' it said. 'Christovao Santos is the best, Em. Straight up, honest, and fair. I'm trusting my life, and yours, to him. Now, what happened to your face?'

'I ran into two very nasty men who were searching the flat. And don't call me Em!' she added, not in a whisper. She punched him, like the old days, high on his left arm.

He cried out, grabbing his left shoulder. His skin paled beneath the dirt on his face and he swayed.

'James!' She reached out for him just as he fell toward her.

Several things happened next in such rapid succession that they felt nearly simultaneous. She went down under James's dead weight, cushioning his fall but ending up sandwiched between him and the deeply padded thick carpet like cheese in a sandwich. When they hit the floor, her remaining breath expelled in a whoosh, leaving her winded. And the fitting room door crashed open.

She looked past James's right shoulder to see Chris, in a towering rage, standing over them.

# 6

Altogether, he was a terrifying sight, with his face twisted and white with fury and his teeth bared. She wanted to tell him that James was hurt but she hadn't the breath.

'*Bastardo!*' Chris ground out between clenched jaws. 'Get away from her, you filthy pig!'

With his left hand he grabbed the back of James's collar and hauled him off her. He held him, with James's feet brushing the carpet, and shook him, his right fist drawn back to deliver a smashing blow.

That gave her the strength to sit up and, since Chris was the only one standing on his own, wrap both arms around the nearest leg. 'It's James,' she gasped.

She had regained enough breath to rasp those two words. She had none left to address the circle of female faces, with eyes agog and mouths moving, that crowded the doorway of the fitting room. Instead, she crawled over and slammed the door. She turned and collapsed against it because she didn't have the strength to stand up.

A padded brocade bench sat along one side

94

of the room. She watched Chris sling James onto the bench and prop him against the wall. By now, James's left arm was red and shiny with fresh blood. Oh, God, what had she done to her brother?

Then Chris turned to her, taking in her bloodied blouse and the length of her bare legs. 'Are you hurt?'

Tears were close. Very close. 'I'm okay. I-it's James's blood.'

He pulled her to her feet with enough force that she could have vaulted right over his head. 'What the hell happened in here?'

'H-he dropped from the ceiling into the room with me. He wanted me to call you in. He seemed okay, then I — There's so much blood. Will he — ?'

'Put your slacks on,' he said, his voice hoarse and shaking, his gaze fixed on the scarlet stain vivid against her white shirt.

She didn't move as she watched *his* blood drain away from his face, leaving his tawny skin a lighter shade. He rested his forearm on the door and leaned his forehead against it for several moments. She had no words, knowing only that she wanted to comfort him, to bring him back here where she and James needed him. She put her hand lightly on his back and rubbed, up and down, as she'd seen mothers do to comfort their babies. He was in control again when he stood upright.

'Flashback,' he said softly as a timid knock sounded at the door. 'Take the clerks and the clothes to the checkout then wait inside at the front of the store. Don't come out unless you can see the Land Rover. And don't ask any questions. Or answer any,' he added when she opened her mouth.

'Give each of them a big tip, for the mess. The show was free.' He shoved his wallet at her and handed her the slacks she'd worn into the fitting room. While she pulled them on, leaning against the wall for support, he jammed her hat and sunglasses into her bag. He gave it to her then piled the clothes into her arms. The shoes she'd worn were balanced on top of the heap.

This sequence of activities was punctuated by one word she uttered over and over again, her gaze fastened on James. 'But . . . but . . . but . . . '

Chris took her by the shoulders and made her look at him. 'He'll be fine, or he wouldn't have made it this far. I'll take him out the back. One of my men is there. We'll see you at the Land Rover. Now go!' He opened the door and shoved her out into the waiting cluster of clerks, smacking her on the bottom as he did so.

The clerks followed her in a flock to the

checkout area. One of the women spoke a little English and was appointed by the others to seek an explanation. Two words floated to the surface of Emily's numbed brain.

'Love triangle,' she croaked.

She put on her shoes while the word duo was translated with relish. The explanation lasted much longer than it would have taken to say 'love triangle' in Portuguese.

The checkout procedure was surreal. The women's and girls' mouths moved in synchronized motion with their hands, which rang up and bagged the merchandise in record time. Emily was aware that some hands also measured what looked like heights and shoulder widths in the air around them.

When she leaned forward to let them scan the tag on the stained blouse she still wore, she realized they really were comparing the physical merits of each of the men who had been with her in the fitting room. She had the feeling the local boy was winning. For that reason, she was very generous with Christovao Santos's money. Thanking the women, she pulled on her new cardigan sweater to cover the bloodstain on her blouse, slapped her hat and sunglasses on, and gathered up her numerous shopping bags.

The Land Rover, motor running, sat farther down the block in a space between the pickups. James sat more or less upright in the backseat on the driver's side. She climbed in beside him, tossing her purchases over the seat into the cargo area. She reached forward and dropped Chris's wallet onto the front passenger seat. In a coordinated move, the pickups angled out into the traffic lane, the one in the rear conveniently stalling out and stopping traffic, which allowed Chris to swing the Land Rover into the space behind the lead pickup. The second pickup's engine sprang to life and they were off.

Emily touched James's good arm. 'James, I'm so sorry I hurt you. I didn't realize you were injured.'

'How did you hurt him? You didn't shoot him, did you?' Chris's eyes met hers in the rearview mirror, which he had adjusted so he could watch them.

She gasped. 'If that's what's wrong with him then it probably felt like I did. I punched his arm because he called me Em.' The tears flowed now, and she let them.

She thought Chris smiled, but he slipped on his sunglasses and looked away so she wasn't sure. James didn't react or answer her. He slumped with his head back against the seat and his eyes closed.

'He'll be okay. He's weak and groggy from blood loss. Sami will pump him full of antibiotics to prevent infection and full of chicken soup for strength, since Mei makes and freezes gallons of the stuff for anyone who gets hurt on the farm. Once we're out of the city, we'll stop, clean him up, see what we have, and make him more comfortable.'

'But aren't we taking him to a hospital?' Her voice rose on the words.

He met her gaze in the rearview mirror. 'Calm down. He said it's a clean bullet wound that goes straight through the fleshy part of his outer arm. Any hospital and most doctors, even in Brazil, would report a bullet wound to the police.'

'And if I insist that you take him to a hospital?'

'You won't,' he said simply. His tone of voice warned her not to press the point, while a stranger glared at her through the dark lenses.

She'd bought a bottle of water in the drugstore. She held it to James's lips and was relieved when he drank deeply.

As soon as they were far enough out of town that the roads were less busy, Chris flicked on the turn signal to pull over. The synchronized pickups fell into place, fore and aft, and the men climbed out, their eyes busy. She got a good look at them for the first time.

Other than an excess of dirt on his face and

hands, in the fitting room James had looked and acted shockingly like their bodyguards. No wonder she hadn't recognized him until he smiled and spoke. They weren't tall like James and Chris, but they carried themselves well and their hair was neatly trimmed when they took off their hats to wipe their brows. James had mimicked their scowls and cold stares perfectly. He even had managed to look a little more dangerous than they looked now as they silently dared anyone to stop to offer assistance or to ask idle questions.

Chris opened the Land Rover's door on the side away from the highway and half-lifted, half-dragged James out onto the grass verge. With a sharp pocketknife, he sliced away the tattered, dirty, blood-soaked work shirt and the T-shirt beneath it. By that time she had found and opened the first-aid kit from the Land Rover.

She handed Chris what he needed or asked for while he cleaned the rather neat wound in the large muscle of James's upper arm. After he fixed a wad of gauze over it, he rolled James over. Emily had been fine up to that point. Now, she was nearly sick in the soft grass when she saw the ragged exit wound in her brother's flesh on the back of his arm.

'Easy, nurse.' He covered her hand briefly

with his bloody one. 'Don't go wobbly on me now. I need you.'

The effect of Chris's words and touch made her take a deep breath and get down to business again. Besides, she would do anything to help her brother — and dare anyone to try to stop her. James was asleep a few minutes after Chris helped him stretch out on the backseat with one of her shopping bags for a pillow. She slid in beside Chris in the front.

She was shocked when he reached out and squeezed her trembling hand that rested on her thigh. She instinctively turned over her hand and laced her fingers tightly with his. He looked down at their clasped hands before he spoke.

'You did well, Emily Noble. Most people never see what a bullet does to human flesh.'

'I hope I never see it again, especially on someone I love.'

'Do you realize that's the first you've spoken in an hour or more? I can't stand the silence.' He smiled, dimple and all.

She ignored it, dimple and all. 'Did he say what happened?'

'He was ambushed in Brasilia. It would have been put down as a mugging gone wrong. He made his way to Barreiras, disguised as a farmworker and used different cyber cafes to send those e-mails to Abundancia. He got here yesterday. He was arranging a ride when he heard on the ex-military grapevine that I was in town this morning with a woman. You. He found out where we were and thought he'd better make contact quietly.'

He stopped and shot a wry look in her direction. 'That didn't work out too well. And I had no idea my movements or personal life were of such interest in this town.'

'It would have worked fine if I hadn't punched him.' She had reached the exhausted reaction stage and was quiet for a moment. 'If the gossip mills grind that efficiently about you, then my hat and sunglasses won't have done much good. You'll have to remember that the next time you're seen around Barreiras in the morning with a woman.'

'I'll keep it in mind. Now, I need that hand to shift, please, or that farm truck ahead will have three Abundancia vehicles up its tailpipe.'

Sami came running when Chris honked the horn as they passed between the big wooden gates into Abundancia's outer compound. James was able to walk, with help, to the bedroom beside hers, where Sami redid, with confidence, what they had done along the road. He added a large shot of antibiotics and a tetanus shot to his treatment.

Emily used that time to put her stained blouse to soak in cold water in her bathtub and to run to the kitchen to ask Mei for chicken soup. A worried Luiz brought the soup just as Sami finished up.

'We'll take it from here, Emily,' James said softly.

'Why don't you take a rest until dinner?' Chris suggested.

She ignored their unsubtle hints and grimly arranged pillows behind James's back, preparing to feed him spoonfuls of hot chicken soup whether he wanted it or not. 'I'm not leaving James for a while.'

She was aware of Chris and Sami exchanging glances then moving toward the door. She was also aware that they stopped dead at the sound of her voice.

'There's no need to tiptoe around me. I'm not going to have hysterics. And don't you think it's time we compare notes, now that we're together and James is safe? I know you can't wait to debrief him or whatever you call it, so if you can't get your minds around my being here, just think of me as the little woman administering healing soup to the patient.' She did just that since James's mouth was hanging open anyway.

'When you want me to tell him *everything*

that happened in London, let me know. The point is, I'm not leaving my brother, so may we please get on with it?'

They turned as one man. James, having dutifully swallowed, watched them, a grin on his face.

'Is she always like this?' Chris asked in a voice thick with amazement.

'Always,' James replied. 'When something's troubling her, anyway. She worries at it until it runs away.'

'I put it down to nerves. How the hell do you stand it?'

'She's usually at a distance these days. Which reminds me. Why did you say you're in Brazil, E.T.? And what really happened in London?' he added. 'I can't seem to remember what you told me in the fitting room.'

She deftly slid in another spoonful. 'Why am I in Brazil? Don't be dense, James. You disappeared. Your secretary didn't even know where you'd gone. For years you've drilled into me that if anything suspicious happened to you, I should look up Christovao Santos in Brazil.'

'So I did. But I e-mailed you explaining that I'd be away for a while, and that I'd be in touch as soon as I got back. Why panic this time?'

'I didn't panic, thank you very much. I never got an e-mail from you explaining that or anything else before I left the States. Look at it from my point of view, James. You dropped out of sight after you informed me that you tripped down the stairs, that you almost stepped into a lift that wasn't there, that a man who intended to stab you mugged you at knifepoint, and that someone almost ran you down in the street. In the meantime, you stopped answering my calls and e-mails. In fact, you blocked me from your e-mail.'

'Did not!'

'Did, too!'

'Children!' Chris's voice thundered.

Emily dropped the spoon into the soup, splashing the leg of her borrowed slacks. 'Look what I've done, and they don't belong to me! There was no need to shout, you know.'

He leaned around a bed poster and she was in his crosshairs. 'I can shout if I damn well please. And I can lock you in your room until you run out of chocolate, lipstick, and moisturizer, if I damn well please.'

Her eyes meshed with his and no one else was in the room. 'I know you can,' she said softly, 'but I'm asking you not to.' Gentleness crept into her voice. 'Force, vocal or physical, isn't the answer in every situation, even for a soldier. Some things, important things, are freely given, you know.'

His knuckles whitened where he gripped the poster, and his eyes narrowed as he studied her.

She sat up straight in her chair and made her voice less personal. 'I'm asking you to let me stay and contribute information or insights, if I can. Please. I might turn out to be an asset instead of the liability you think I am. Besides, isn't teamwork essential in situations like this?'

He held her gaze a moment longer then jerked his head in acknowledgment. 'Oh, always. It gives the enemy someone else to shoot at.' Then he pointed his index finger at her. 'Just remember you're here on sufferance, by association. You are *not* an active player.'

He went to the door and asked the guard to get two chairs from somewhere. She mashed up the noodles and bits of vegetables in the soup and placed the cup in James's right hand so he could sip it. When the chairs came, Chris and Sami set them on the other side of the bed, putting James between her and them.

Chris wasted no time. 'You need to know some facts, James, if you don't know them already. Smitty, Duke, O'Reilly, Turk, and

DelGrosso are dead. All accidents, all within the last month.'

'Bloody hell.' James's face turned a pasty white. 'I just saw Turk about eight weeks ago. He stayed at the flat for a few nights. He was jumpy as hell. He kept looking out the windows and refused to go out.'

'Turk was here, too, about six weeks ago. He was kind of skittish, now that you mention it. Maybe he'd had accidents, too. Since then he and the others have died, you've had accidents, and I've had vandalism and an accident. And Emily was assaulted by two men in your London flat.'

'What?' James set the cup on the nightstand and groped for Emily's hand. 'Your face?'

She nodded. 'I came to London to find you. I walked in on them while they were searching the flat. They thought I might know where you had gone or where some papers they wanted might be. One of them read my name on my passport and knew somehow that I was your sister. They were going to take me with them but I got away.'

'You didn't tell me about any papers, or that they knew who you were from your name, or that they were going to kidnap you.' Chris's eyes burned like violet flames across the bed.

'I just remembered the last bit. And as I recall, you gave me an edited version of things because you didn't trust me. James had vouched for you, in a way, but I didn't trust you, either.' Her head was beginning to pound.

'How did you get away?' James asked, curiosity apparently getting the better of him.

She smiled. 'You would have been proud. I used the self-defense training you taught me all those years ago. When the tall one went off to find something to gag me and tie my hands, I punched the short one in the throat and kicked him in the — , um, disabled the short one, grabbed my bags, went straight back to the airport, and came here.'

Sami stifled a sound. It took her a moment to figure out he was laughing.

'Tell me exactly what they said to each other when they realized you were James's sister. No more holding back, Emily. This could be important.' Chris's intense stare made her want to please him, but it also made it hard for her to concentrate.

She leaned back in the upholstered chair and thought. 'The tall one scarcely spoke at all. He just . . . watched me. The short one went through my purse, took my cash, and read my name on my passport. He poked the tall one with his elbow. 'Hey, it's Emily

Noble, the sister. It worked.' ' She stopped and took a deep breath. 'Then he added, 'They'll both come running.' The other one, the tall one, didn't react at all to the information.'

Her face grew hot when she recalled the shorter man's next words, the tall one's instant, angry response, and what happened to her when his anger turned on her.

Chris's voice hissed across her embarrassment like cold water on hot metal. 'There's more. What is it?'

She looked away from all of them. 'What was said next had nothing to do with this, but everything to do with me, as a woman.'

James hadn't finished his soup. When she reached for the cup to give her hands something to do, he grasped her wrist. She looked up and her breath caught. A warrior watched her through her brother's eyes.

'You'll tell us now or you'll tell me when you and I are alone, but you *will* tell one of us what he said to you, Emily,' he told her quietly.

'Leave it for now, James,' Chris said in a low, intense voice. 'Can you describe these men?'

'They wore black ski masks, black pants, and black turtlenecks. The tall one was most definitely in charge. He was slim and he moved well, efficiently. He reminded me . . . of a soldier, I guess. He spoke very little but when he did, his voice was a hoarse whisper, with the slightest hint of an accent, like he was disguising it. I remember that the short one looked at him in surprise the first time he spoke after I came in. The little one was cockney. Stocky. Compact. With brown eyes.'

'Probably local talent,' Chris commented. 'What about the tall one's eyes?'

'His were creepy, a light gray or such a washed-out blue that they looked almost colorless against the black mask . . . ' Her voice died away when the three men silently looked at each other in turn.

Sami spoke first. His voice wasn't velvet now. 'Impossible. He's dead.'

'Nothing's impossible with that bastard,' Chris added.

'Dutch?' James asked in an amazed, doubting tone.

'Who's Dutch?' Emily slipped in her question, hoping someone would speak without thinking first.

James opened his mouth to answer her.

Chris headed him off. 'She knows all she needs to know, James. If I find out you've told her more, I swear I'll shoot you in the other arm.'

# 7

She pinned Chris to his chair with a look. 'And we were all playing so well together.'

James had gone still, watching her. 'I think I'd like to hear now what this tall man with the strange eyes said to you, Em,' he whispered.

'Don't call me Em!' There wasn't much fight in the words.

She felt three sets of eyes on her, a violet pair, a brown pair, and a black pair. Waiting.

'The short one asked if he could . . . have me, when I wasn't needed anymore. The tall one you call Dutch said he would castrate the little one if he so much as thought of it again. He said I was h-his.'

They managed to keep James, in his weakened state, on the bed, with her holding him on one side and Chris on the other. Sami, his face hard, sat silent and unmoving in his chair, unaware of their struggles.

'At ease, James,' Chris said quietly into James's ear as he strained against their hands, saying horrible things, words she'd never heard before, some of them in strange languages. 'I need you to focus. He's killing off the survivors of Cheneyville, and I'll bet he'll do the grunt work himself on me — on us. Five down, three to go. He'll come after us now — and her. And we'll take him down. But we have to work together because it's too easy for him if we don't. And we don't want to make it easy for him, do we?'

At last, Emily thought, someone had spoken without thinking first. Cheneyville. She mentally scooped up the word and stashed it out of sight until she could think about it, dissect it, research it, understand it, and own it.

She was relieved when James went limp beneath her hands. After a moment she and Chris let go of him. Emily heard someone speak into the thick silence broken only by James's heavy breathing. They all looked at her and she realized the voice was hers.

'If I can be bait for this man who wants to kill you three then dangle me.' She clapped a hand over her mouth to stop it saying anything else as remotely stupid as the words it had just uttered. She met Chris's astonished stare across her brother's legs.

The moment didn't last long before Chris was back to business. 'The short one said 'It worked.' What worked?'

She fell back into her chair, exhausted. 'The fact that I'd come to England, looking for James, when I couldn't reach him?'

Sami spoke, black velvet again. 'She was blocked from James's e-mail. If James didn't do it, then someone hacked into his e-mail accounts and did it. If someone hacked in then they would be able to read everything Emily Noble and James talked about. And they could track James when he logged on to check his messages as he traveled.'

She wondered briefly if everyone at Abundancia thought her full first name was both Emily and Noble. Or maybe they had hyphenated her when she wasn't looking.

Chris's voice cut across the thought. 'Emily leaves a paper trail and James leaves an electronic one, right to Abundancia. I guess X marks the spot. Do you two talk online about being brother and sister?'

She met James's eyes briefly. 'It's no secret that we're brother and sister. James just doesn't talk about me to business associates. But in our e-mails we talk about our parents and about things that happened when we were growing up, and I call him 'bro' or 'little brother' all the time, although he's older than I am and certainly bigger.'

Chris watched her, studied her as she spoke, then his expression changed from one of consideration to cold, heartless calculation. He now looked at her like she was the newest model of one of those huge farm machines in his sheds, estimating how many hours per season he could get out of her, how often she'd break down, how much her spare parts might cost him, and he'd take two dozen in that color.

'She's right. We'll use her, if we have to, when the time is right,' he said, almost to himself.

Everyone spoke at once but Emily was sure her voice was the loudest. 'M-maybe we should think about this some more.'

'You're not using my sister for bait, Hawk.'

'You know what he's capable of. We can't use Emily Noble!'

It was her turn again. 'Hawk? Why are you called Hawk?'

Chris ignored them. His eyes remained fixed on her. 'Not just her, all of us. Sami can put support behind every bush, surrounding us with a wall of protection. As soon as we're sure the bastard's here, we'll set something up, and hope he's so pumped by the opportunity to take out three of us at once that he gets careless.'

'And how will we know he's h-here?' Her voice was the voice of a scared little girl.

Chris stood up and stretched. 'Because he'll tell us. Since we're giving him so much trouble, I'm betting he'll want us to know it's him before we die. If he wants to grandstand this, we'll give him his chance. He'll be deadly then, but that's also when he's apt to slip up.'

Chris paid no attention to their indignant, sputtered questions and headed for the door, declaring he was returning to the work he'd let slide for days.

★ ★ ★

Emily didn't waste any time. Once James fell asleep, she went in search of books. Atlases and geographies were well-represented in Chris's library. She pounced on them. Cheneyville wasn't mentioned, and she concluded that it was too small or was known by another name in another language.

She took time to glance over the rest of Chris's small, neat collection. Histories, language books, military strategy, logistics, and tactics were much in evidence. A few biographies, classics, and fiction rounded out the collection. She saw no rhyme or reason in the arrangement of the books, but felt sure Chris had a system she simply couldn't see. She was careful to reshelve the books she'd pulled in their correct place.

She didn't find anything in the books in the other rooms in the house that were open to her, and she didn't have the courage to sneak into or casually stroll undetected into Chris's bedroom next door to hers to look for books. The thought of him finding her there, after the clothes incident, very nearly sent her into a fetal position.

She desperately wanted to research Cheneyville on the Internet, but the computer was in Chris's study, and Sami worked in that room most of the time. She wouldn't ask to use it because with her trail-leaving history, probably neither Chris nor Sami would let her near Abundancia's computer.

She didn't yet know how Sami fit into the household. He wasn't a servant or an employee, but he was certainly Chris's and James's friend. They treated him with respect and, when he spoke, they listened. Though he was always polite to her, something in his eyes stopped her from getting too close or asking questions. Although she'd learned to relax around Sami, wherever she ran into him, her friendly overtures were gently rebuffed.

That wasn't the case with the guards. Things settled into a kind of routine, and she got to know her door guard very well over the next tense week.

'I'll introduce myself, since no one else has bothered,' she told him on the first day. 'I'm

Emily Noble, James King's sister.'

'Manoel, *senhorita*,' he'd answered in halting speech. He clasped the hand she extended to him then quickly let it go.

'It looks like we'll be spending some time together, Manoel. You were a soldier?' His eyes weren't quite . . . even . . . so she picked one and concentrated on it.

He noticed. '*Sim*, a soldier. It is fake, *senhorita*, the left one. The *patrao* bought it for me. Would you like to see?' He eagerly shrugged his gun strap over his shoulder.

'No!' She held up a hand. 'Thank you. It was very kind of the *patrao* to do that for you.'

He smiled, taking no offense at her squeamishness. 'He is good. And I am very lucky it was my left eye I lost.'

This man was his own spin doctor if he could turn such a tragedy into something positive. 'Oh? Why is that?'

'I am . . . ' He paused, searching for the words. He found them. 'Senhor James explained it to me. I am right-eyed when I aim a gun, *senhorita*. And I am the best shot on all of Abundancia.'

She guessed that made her lucky, too, since Chris, in his wisdom, had given her a right-sighted, one-eyed guard who was a crack shot.

Of course, the house now had many guards, and she soon called all of them by name. When she went to the courtyard to draw, the roof guards quietly collected around that side. Every time she looked up, she was met with smiles, waves, and hearty greetings. She chose one of them each day to help her with her Portuguese and her atrocious accent.

She learned that their shifts were twelve hours on and twelve hours off. After the first day or so she noticed new faces and asked Manoel about it.

'The night guards asked for daylight time, too.'

'Because of their families?'

'Because of you, senhorita. You are very beautiful and they want to help you with your Portuguese.'

Manoel's position held a certain cachet with the other guards. They held him in high esteem because he had been chosen to be her personal guard. He explained in the course of their conversations that he, a former soldier, was one of Chris's farmworkers when things were normal at Abundancia. She also learned from him that Chris, as she suspected, was generous in many ways with his workers and their families. Signing on as a mercenario still paid more, but here at Abundancia they had lived in peace for many years.

She also discovered Chris's stable and two grazing fields behind it on her accompanied explorations. The building sat some distance behind the house but inside the outer wall. She visited Chris's magnificent black Arabian stallion, Diabo, and his female companions every day, bearing apples or carrots for them, which she cadged from Mei in the kitchen. One new female was kept for breeding, Estrela, a delicate black Arabian beauty made more beautiful by the approaching birth of her first foal.

Other guards began to tag along on these daily walking jaunts. Only Manoel went with her around back to the fence, however. Diabo lived up to his name, Devil, with the guards, although she found him to be almost catlike in his responses to her.

Chris surprised them there once, apparently having dismissed the guards loitering in front of the stable. 'Get back, Emily! What are you doing to my horse?'

She jumped away from Diabo, whose head hung low over the top fence rail, his eyes half-closed. What she had been doing was sweet-talking his stallion. And the stallion liked it.

'I, um, I was just talking to him, that's all.'

He jerked a thumb at Manoel, who swiftly turned to leave them. Chris said something in

Portuguese as he passed, something that made Manoel's whole demeanor change. He almost slunk away.

'Just talking? To a breeding stallion? Nobody can get near that horse except me,' he insisted, despite what he'd seen.

She stepped forward again and Diabo rubbed her stomach with his nose, making little noises. 'He reminds me of Gato. Please don't make me stop visiting him. I visit the mares, too.'

Chris gave a horse-like snort, shaking his head. 'No closer and be careful!' He looked at Diabo, long and hard. 'Traitor,' he said before turning away.

She had no trouble finding other ways to stay occupied. It had taken her less than a day to improvise and gather the rudimentary art supplies available to her so she could draw. Luckily, she always carried colored pencils and a small sharpener in her carry-on bag. She commandeered a ream of copy paper and some soft pencils from Chris's study via Sami. She simply knocked on the study door and asked for the items when he opened it.

With Manoel's help, she found a piece of plywood in an outbuilding. When one edge of it rested in her lap on a folded towel, and its opposite edge rested on the lip of a large flowerpot or against a column, the plywood served as a makeshift drawing board. After that, she spent a lot of time in the courtyard. She thought of anything that took her mind off their situation as mental health work.

Despite the tension, the waiting, the guards, and the guns, she was strangely content spending her days drawing in Abundancia's inner courtyard. She divided the remainder of her time helping Mei where and when Mei permitted, catching up with her brother while he healed, and studying Chris when she caught a glimpse of him. When he wasn't on the land, he spent most of his time with Sami in the study, or with James in his room as long as she wasn't there. She saw him at dinner, but only after James was well enough to join them. She never saw him alone.

One pleasant late afternoon she glanced up from the drawing on her board and was instantly ensnared by his wide-set violet eyes. He pushed away from the column he leaned against, putting him twenty feet away and closing. She wondered how long he'd stood there watching her. When the roof guards caught sight of him, they scattered. He stopped, frowned in their direction, and said something to Manoel. Manoel got up, stretched, and ambled toward the kitchen.

Chris's gaze took a long, slow journey over

the moderate area of skin exposed by her cropped top and hip-hugging shorts, then it flicked back to the roof. 'I warned them about allowing you to distract them. I'll have another word with them.'

She had squirmed under his examination, wondering what a word from Christovao Santos might entail. At his slightly accusing tone, she launched into an explanation. 'When I got the shorts home from Barreiras, I discovered they were low-cut. They're not my choice, but what the clerk gave me. Remember, in the excitement of James dropping in on me, I didn't try them on. At least they're comfortable to work in and they suit the climate.'

As he continued his approach, her artist's eye followed the natural tapering line of his six feet, plus two or three inches, of height. He was what her mother had called a well-knit man, a fine specimen from his big shoulders to his flat stomach to his well-muscled thighs, all encased this day in a sweaty, dirty khaki shirt and matching pants. The shirt, dark where perspiration had soaked in, clung to his chest. His broad-brimmed bush hat shaded his eyes, just as the big, floppy hat she'd worn to Barreiras now shaded hers.

His frown suddenly vanished and he

smiled, making her drop the colored pencil she held. The contrast between white teeth, a day's worth of dark beard, and the smooth, tawny silk of his skin sent a thrill of fear through her. She and James trusted this? Did they have a choice?

'I'm glad you're drawing, keeping busy,' he said when the silence dragged on, broken only by the wind and the tinkling of the fountain. 'The guards have reported that you're very good.'

She picked up the pencil and put it with the others, upright in a coffee mug at her feet beside Gato. 'Reported?'

He looked toward the roof again. 'At shift changes, they tell me how the day went, if there were any incidents, and so on.'

She watched him speak, not really listening, but fascinated as his presence expanded, somehow filling the open courtyard. He ruled this land, this house, these men, this little corner of the world in every sense of the word. With a graceful sweep, he removed his hat and tossed it onto a mosaic-topped table. His long, graceful fingers combed through his already neat hair.

Ever since her first, fever-ridden look at him in his study, she'd tried, unsuccessfully, to gauge the exact color of his eyes. In this light and on this day, she finally settled on

English violets, drenched in sunlight.

'I see.' She wondered if the guards would leave out of this day's report that three of them left the roof to join her and Manoel on their little walk around the compound that morning. 'I'm ready to stop for the day.'

She stood up, cramped from hours of sitting still. She tried to take a break every hour or so, but six and a half sets of male eyes watching her every move hindered her stretches. Usually she retreated to her room to do them.

She placed the plywood on the wooden bar stool she'd borrowed from Mei then sailed her hat like a flying disk onto the table beside his.

He watched the hat's graceful arc, then his eyes moved from the top of her fair head to her bare feet, as she briefly lifted each leg behind her and flexed her fingers.

'You were smiling when I came out.'

'Ah, my secret's out. Don't tell anyone, but I enjoy what I do more than I'm willing to let people know.'

'Did I hear you correctly when you woke up from your fever? You illustrate children's books?'

'You sound surprised.'

'Just because I've never met a children's book illustrator before. Are they all like you?'

She put her hands on her hips. 'That question is very much like the 'Have you stopped beating your wife?' one.'

He motioned toward her makeshift drawing board. 'Okay, then, tell me how you do . . . what you do.'

She felt a grin start. 'You asked for it. I think of the process as magical, or at least it feels that way sometimes. It begins when I'm assigned a book. I get what's called a black-and-white dummy board from Tot's Press. It shows the layout of the text on the pages and where the illustrations will go. I draw in my interpretation of the story on it, using suggestions from the author and the art director. When it's finished, I discuss changes with the art director and the editor and sometimes with the publisher. Then I do the final layout in color, incorporating any changes we've agreed upon.'

She paused to look at him closely. 'I knew it. Your eyes are glazing over. Seriously, I'm between books right now, thank heavens, or I'd be wild with worry about meeting my deadline.'

He leaned down to look at the paper she'd pinned to the plywood. She caught his scent, an exhilarating, disturbing mixture of green living things, perspiration, exhaust fumes, and soap.

'It's Manoel. Are you giving this to him? His wife would be pleased. It's just like him.'

She was glad he liked the sketch because she thought she'd captured Manoel rather well, not just the ex-soldier's ravaged, hardened, physical appearance but also the humor, pride, and determination of the man behind the face.

'Yes, I meant to ask you if it would be all right to offer it. And you sound surprised again.'

He shoved his hands into his pants pockets, looking at the closed folder of drawings nearby. 'It's admiration, not surprise. I have to use a ruler to draw a straight line.'

She was thankful that the many sketches she'd done of him were in her room. She'd used up all her violet and purple pencils on those eyes. Now, her fingers itched to capture more of the man, the essence of *this* man, on paper.

'Will you pose for me sometime?' She bit her lip but it was too late to call back the words, the fantasy.

He went still, his face losing its smile. 'Pose for you?'

She gathered up the other drawings she'd worked on that day. 'You're looking at me as though I've just asked you to do something incredibly rude. I'll rephrase it. Will you pose for me sometime, please? Clothed,' she added with a grin.

He shook his head. 'No, thanks. I don't have time to pose for anybody. Besides, I'd feel a fool.'

She nodded her acceptance of his decision. 'That's not an unusual reaction. Many people feel that way.' She changed the subject by opening the folder and showing him drawings she'd done of Gato. 'These are the many faces of Gato.'

He glanced down at his cat, who had spent the afternoon sleeping at her feet. Gato was halfway turned over onto his back with one paw curled over his eyes. His dark stripes and white belly stood out in contrast against the old pink bath towel she'd found in her bathroom linen closet.

'If you won't pose for me, you can at least tell me about your cat. He might star in his own children's book one day, with your permission. How do you like the title *Gato of the Cerrados*?'

His eyes sparkled although he didn't smile outright. 'I like it a lot better than *Christovao of the Cerrados*. I found him in an alley one dark, rainy night in Barreiras, near Paulo's dance club. He was battle-weary like me. He had scars like me. He looked like he could use a little peace, a sanctuary.'

'Like you?' she asked softly.

He didn't hear, or he pretended he didn't. 'I called a vet out of bed to check him out, and I brought him here to live the good life for the rest of his days.'

She'd come to know and appreciate Gato over the past week. Under the attitude, the scars, and all that fur beat the heart of a true warrior who showed no mercy to anything that moved within his territory. Yet he showed her a gentle, charming, humorous side that was at odds with that other part of him. She suspected the cat was very like his master.

'Look at him,' he continued. 'Not a care in the world. He doesn't care who's gunning for us.'

That jolted her back to reality. She followed his lead. 'Any sign of . . . whatever?'

'No. And it's too quiet.' His head came up and she was sure he whiffed the air like a hunted animal. 'That might be part of the plan, though. Make us edgy, give us time to let our guard down.'

'We're edgy but we're not letting our guard down, right?' She couldn't help the little jitter in her voice.

'Right. Don't worry. Unless, of course, you count the roof guards ogling you when they should be scanning the area.'

'You have two on each roof section, right?

When you remind them of their duties shortly, suggest that one of them can ogle while the other watches our backs.'

'Easy for you to say,' he said.

His look and his words launched her on a tangent, her mind settling on a project that had been niggling at her since she arrived. 'I've been thinking and I have a proposition for you, nothing to do with our problem here.'

He went very still. 'I'm listening.'

'I'd like to do a proposal for a children's book, maybe two, about Abundancia, the whole agricultural scene of Western Bahia, in fact. The farm, not you personally,' she quickly added when his face turned wary.

'I'm a good photographer and I'd want to take pictures, follow the crops from planting to harvest to trucking them out. I can draw illustrations from the shots or propose the book as a photo essay for the intermediate age group and as a nonfiction picture book for the kindergarten crowd.

'This is new territory for me, and I don't know if it will fly. I'd have to submit proposals to my publisher, when he gets back from vacation, and get the go-ahead. Will you help me?'

'My cat, my horses, my farm. What's next? Yes, I'll help you. I certainly can't stop you.

You have all the farms of Western Bahia to choose from.'

'You'd have to introduce me to the owners and their families. But I want the books to be mainly about Abundancia. This place is special. You've made it special. You said yourself you'd like it to be the gold standard by which other *cerrados* farms are measured.' Her frustration level soared without warning. 'Now that I've voiced it, I can't wait to get started. How long will we go on like this, putting our lives on hold?'

'As long as it takes,' he replied evenly. 'And be glad you still have a life to put on hold. I know of five men who don't.'

She was instantly contrite. 'You're right. I'm sorry. I was excited. Selfish.'

'You don't appear unhappy.' He hesitated. 'Are you?'

She was aware he watched her closely, so she spoke as truthfully as she could. 'No, don't ever think that. I'm very content here, in fact. That's what I was thinking about before you appeared. This is a beautiful, tranquil place that would be excellent for my work, almost as good as Cornwall.' She smiled in a teasing way. 'You should be thankful, you know. I could be climbing the walls, wanting to go shopping in Barreiras all the time, and making your life a living hell.'

He didn't answer immediately, and when he did his harsh words slapped the smile off her face. 'I went through that with one woman, so what makes you think that having another one under my roof twenty-four hours a day, seven days a week, doesn't *make* my life a living hell?'

He spun around and went back the way he'd come, calling to Manoel as he went.

# 8

For a moment, her lower lip threatened to jut forward in a pout that would precede tears. She bit the pout into submission and fought back the tears. His words had shocked her, but so did her reaction to them. Hurt. She'd thought he at least tolerated her presence, though it might be unwanted, and that maybe he even liked her a little. Why did it matter so much what he thought of her?

One person came to mind who knew the details of what had happened here, who perhaps knew why the mystery woman had left Christovao Santos. She'd never really had that girl talk with Mei. So, she put away her drawing things and sought the counsel of the only other woman within walking distance, and the only one around who might trust her enough to part with delicate information.

Mei had thawed over the past week under Emily's friendly gestures and offers of help. She welcomed her into the *cozinha*, the kitchen, plying her with iced tea and a sympathetic presence.

When they were settled at the kitchen table, Emily decided to ease into confidences by following up on a far-fetched theory that came to her after the council of war around James's bed. If she had thought of it then Chris and the others surely had thought of it, too, although they wouldn't tell her. Had they already asked the one person who might be able to verify it and give them details?

She jumped in. 'Mei, would you like to help fix the trouble that has come to Abundancia? Will you answer a few questions for me?'

The tiny woman nodded her head an emphatic yes.

'When a visitor by the name of Turk was here six weeks ago, which room did he stay in?'

The tiny mouth pulled into a straight, displeased line. 'Supposed to stay in Mr. James's room.'

Emily felt a frisson of excitement. 'Supposed to? Did he move to another bedroom?'

'No. But no stay where supposed to. I find him in the woman's room. Your room. Two times. I keep all rooms clean.'

She cautioned herself not to get excited. Maybe Turk had a fetish for women's clothing. Or maybe he liked the ambience and the bathroom in her room. Her bedroom was much nicer than James's room.

'What was he doing there?'

'First time sitting in chair. Pouch open on knees.'

'Pouch? What do you mean?'

'Pouch for papers. Flat. Zipper all around.'

'A portfolio. What did he do when you found him? Did he explain what he was doing in there?'

She shook her head. 'Shove papers in pouch. Close pouch. Leave room. I see him coming out of room another time. Then I lock room until he leave the next day.'

'Did he have the pouch with him the second time you saw him?'

'No pouch.'

'Did you find the pouch in any of the other rooms after he left?'

Again she shook her head. 'No see again.'

A nervous Turk had visited James before he visited Chris. He had been in the woman's room — er, her room — at least twice while he was here. Mei had seen him with a portfolio and papers. The men in James's flat were looking for papers. What if Turk had whatever those men wanted? What if he had brought it here and hid it in her room? He would have known visitors never stayed in it, until she stumbled on the scene, after he had died.

Mei sat quietly while Emily waded through her convoluted thoughts. Then she spoke, driving Turk and his portfolio right out of Emily's mind.

'Sami put you in the woman's room. The *patrao* very angry. But he let you stay. It is good.' She nodded sagely.

Emily's shock tied her thoughts and her tongue into knots. 'It is? Good? Why is it good?'

'You can get the woman out of the *patrao*'s head, Sami says.'

Emily shook her own head to clear it. If she didn't regain control of this conversation, she wouldn't know anything useful about the mystery woman when she left.

'Who was she, Mei? Why did she run away?'

'The *patrao* love Maria Pandolfo. She his *noiva*. Fiancée. Love deep. She hate Abundancia. Run off with a Rio man. *Patrao* proud man — '

Mei's gasp and wild look made Emily squeak and twist around in her chair to see what horror lay behind her. Christovao Santos stood in the kitchen doorway. Of course, it would be him when she would have much preferred a horror that hadn't overheard what Mei had just said about his pride and his humiliation.

Three steps led down into the room. Chris stood on the landing at the top, outlined by the screened door behind him, watching them with eyes so icy purple that she shivered. She and Mei silently returned his stare like guilty children. When Emily stood to face him, and the music, Mei broke the thick silence with a flurry of Chinese words, accompanied by frantic shooing gestures.

Chris silenced his cook with one word. He leisurely descended the steps and walked up to Emily. She almost abandoned her dignity and ran to James, who was in the study with Sami, for protection. Her mouth opened and closed but nothing useful came out. She'd been caught gossiping about him. She couldn't defend that.

'You have colored pencil smudges on your cheek.' He lightly brushed at the spot, holding her head with his other hand when she flinched. Then he turned to Mei and spoke in Portuguese. Emily realized he was giving his cook a royal chewing out, and that she was the cause of it. Guilt over-came caution.

'Chris, please,' she said. 'Don't be angry with her. This conversation, which turned into a gossip session, is my fault.'

'I never doubted it.' With an abrupt gesture, he signaled that she should precede him up the stairs and out of the kitchen. Now.

She sighed. 'Let me guess. You'd like a word with me in the *sala*, wouldn't you?'

In the sitting area she sat down in one of the overstuffed chairs and watched him pace for a few minutes before she spoke, keeping her voice gentle, as if calming a wild animal. 'Mei talks to me sometimes, Chris. She's frightened and lonely. Her quiet world here has been turned upside down lately. She wants another woman's company, someone to explain — '

He turned on her, his vicious tone making her wince. 'If you have any answers, perhaps you'd be good enough to explain a few things to me. Don't forget this is my peaceful world, too, that's been shot to hell.'

How could she ever express her shame? 'I apologize to you, Chris, sincerely and deeply, and I'll apologize to Mei for encouraging her to gossip.' Gato hopped up onto her lap. She buried her fingers in his thick fur.

'It's a start,' Chris said as he passed behind her chair.

'You suspected I had no manners when you found me trying on the clothes from the closet in my room. Today I've violated your hospitality a second time. I'm very, very sorry. James will probably beat me if you ask him nicely.'

He stepped in front of her, putting one

hand on each arm of her chair and his face close to hers. She pressed back against the upholstered cushion as far as she could. She wouldn't mind Chris getting closer, but not when he was in a temper.

'How do you do it?' He looked down at Gato, who looked back. And growled. 'My horse, my guards, even my damned cat. How the *hell* do you do it?' Amazement was thick in his whispered words.

'D-do what?'

He stood upright, shoved the game table out of his way with one booted foot, and started pacing again, this time between her chair and its mate. 'I swore no woman would ever set foot in this house again, except my mother and a little Chinese cook who's had a hard life and needs a break. Then you descended on me, taming and laying claim to everyone and everything in my world.'

He paused, his breath coming fast and shallow. 'My guards, most of them former hard-core soldiers pressed back into service for the duration of this mess, turn into friendly puppies when you're near them. Sami, who never responds to anyone, takes one look at you and says you're the one who will exorcise my demons, whatever the hell that means. Mei tells you things she has no right, out of respect for me, to tell anyone.

She won't even let me inside her damned kitchen, *my* kitchen, but I find *you* in there drinking tea!'

She gathered up Gato and jumped to her feet, meeting Chris face-to-face on his return trip. 'I'm sorry and it won't happen again. What more can I say? What can I say or do to make it right? Tell me, but for heaven's sake, don't go on and on about whatever it is you imagine I've done, over and above gossiping with your cook.'

She stopped and forced a deep breath. 'This is me, Chris,' she said. 'This is the way I am. I talk to people. I make friends. I bloom where I'm planted, and right now I'm planted at Abundancia because some maniac wants you and my brother and Sami dead.'

His voice was clear, cold, and as cutting as the ice in his eyes. 'Just stay away from my people while you're here and we won't have any problems. Don't. Make. Friends.'

'Fine. Is there anything else, or may I go now? Let's see. It hasn't rained since I arrived. The guards talk endlessly about the *vecancio* and whether or when you'll irrigate. Is the *vecancio* my fault, too? I suppose I bellied up to the rain gods and said, 'My life and that of my brother depend on this man and his resources. This beautiful place he loves is our refuge, our sanctuary. How can I get up his nose so he doesn't want me here? I know! Help me dry up his crops.' '

She was running out of anger and patience. 'Just send me away. Please. Anywhere will do. Then you can have your little world and your memories all to yourself again.'

His mask slipped and she saw anguish. 'I don't want you to . . . ' His tortured words trailed off.

He took a step toward her at the same moment James appeared in the doorway, edging in. Sami was behind him, edging in a much larger way.

'Er, problems, Em?'

'Don't call me Em!' She took a deep breath and regained control of herself and her voice. 'I did something wrong, Chris caught me, and I apologized. It's all a blur after that. Surely you've heard this man yelling at someone before now?'

James and Sami exchanged looks. 'Of course. It's just that nobody ever yelled back.'

She brushed past them on her way out the door. 'Well, it's about time someone did.'

She heard Chris's threat as she stalked away. And she heard James's conciliatory noises.

'If he doesn't make a move on one of us soon, I'm going to strangle your sister, James!'

'Emily has this effect on people sometimes, Hawk. When she hurls truths at you, just ignore her. That's what I do.'

She wondered if she could make it legal and divorce James as her brother. To merely disown him lacked a certain cachet she was looking for.

She stopped just inside her bedroom doorway, put Gato down, and studied the area while her breathing returned to normal.

The walls were painted a soft cream color that complemented the sage green, lavender, and cream in the mixture of floral-print and solid materials used for cushions, draperies, the bed covering, and chair.

The cozy wing chair, a small table, a floor lamp for reading, and a footstool shared an area rug. She thought of it as the library corner because behind the chair was a built-in bookcase. A fruitwood bureau, a dressing table and slipper chair, and a delicate antique desk and chair were positioned around the large, airy room. Most of the wall on one side of the bed was devoted to the closet that had gotten her into so much trouble. An overhead fan quietly and efficiently created a breeze. Chris had told her that heating and air conditioning were not needed in the *cerrados*.

If she wanted to hide something in this

room, where would she put it? Correction. If a man wanted to hide something in this room, where would he put it? The hiding place would either be ridiculously obvious or frustratingly difficult, involving tools to uncover it. Her gaze settled on the contents of the bookcase as obvious. Were the papers still in the portfolio, shoved behind the books? Although she'd gotten sidetracked and had leafed through many of these books when looking for information about Cheneyville, she decided to do it thoroughly and started over.

She hadn't gotten far, removing each book, fanning through it, and checking behind it in the case, before she had to stop to get ready for dinner. She showered and then pulled out one of her skirts and her sandals. She decided which regular-length T-shirt and which embroidered blouse to wear open over it. Somehow, Mei had gotten out the blood-stains, so she still had three embroidered blouses to choose from. What her wardrobe lacked in quantity, it made up for in monotony.

Chris was behind the bar mixing drinks when she went into the *sala*. His eyes snagged hers and held. She'd be polite, and quiet, if it killed her.

'Good evening,' she said and sat down

beside James on the loveseat. Sami had joined them tonight and he and James were engaged in a chess match. The game table had been moved back to the center of the seating area, between the sofa and loveseat. She leaned forward to study the game's progress thus far.

'Would you like something?' Chris's voice was strained.

'Yes, please. A sherry would be lovely, thank you.'

She thanked him again when he handed her the drink a minute later. The tiny glass was halfway to her lips when she noticed a muscle working in Chris's jaw as he served the others their drinks. He sat down beside Sami, who drank fruit juice, on the sofa opposite her and James.

'We've been talking. Can you tell us more about the men in the flat? Any little thing at all?' James asked. 'We can't assume it's Dutch based simply on eye color and height, you see.'

Chris's voice played on her nerves. 'We're not getting anything useful from our contacts or from the families of the men who have died. They haven't seen anyone with white hair and pale eyes.'

She continued to study the chessboard, avoiding Chris's piercing stare. 'That's not surprising. With that coloring he could

143

change his appearance easily with hair dye and tinted contact lenses. And there's always cosmetic surgery.'

'Not cosmetic surgery. Not Dutch,' Chris continued. 'He's a vain bastard. He fancies himself as some ice god or something.'

Her gaze flicked up to Sami when he spoke, his voice as smooth as her sherry. 'Can you draw any detail about them, Emily Noble, since you could not see their faces?' He pulled a small white pad and a regular pencil from the space between the side of the sofa and his massive thigh.

She put down her drink and took the pad and pencil. 'I'll try, Sami.'

Something hovered, just on the edge of her memory. She let it sidle in, her pencil moving where it would. And there it was in black-and-white, the dream that had plagued her and played behind her eyes so many nights. She had drawn the tall one with his left arm folded across his chest to deliver a brain-numbing, backhanded slap.

She turned the pad toward Chris. 'He was left-handed! The one you call Dutch back-handed me with his left hand when I made him angry.' She imitated his movement, folding her left arm across her chest then lashing out with it. 'That's why my *left* cheek and eye were bruised.'

Chris's features turned wooden. 'Dutch is left-handed.'

'You made him angry, Emily? Not a good idea.' James's voice held concern mixed with exasperation. 'Dutch never had a sense of humor. You didn't kick him, too?'

'He still doesn't have a sense of humor, but, no, I didn't kick him. After the, um, exchange I repeated for you after we got home from Barreiras, I said something extremely rude to him. And he reacted.' She felt her face grow warm at the same time a shiver rippled over her.

'Good Lord,' James muttered, watching her. 'You were face-to-face with a vicious murderer, sister of mine. Tell me what you said.'

'Never, James. You'd look into disowning me, instead of the other way around.'

Chris watched her closely, his jaws clenched. 'Anything else?'

She closed her eyes, as much to get away from those eyes as to replay the scene in her head, which was something she avoided in her waking hours.

Her eyes popped open. 'A ring.'

Her pencil moved on a fresh sheet of paper as quickly as her mouth had formed her words. She handed the pad to Chris.

'He wore that ring on his other hand, his

right hand. It was jade, I think, with a Chinese symbol in gold inlay or as a cage-like covering over the stone.'

The room was so quiet she heard the fountain's melody and the wind ruffling the plants in the courtyard.

'It *is* Dutch. That cunning bastard.' Chris muttered the words and packed them in ice.

Sami spoke, his eyes fastened on her drawing, with no inflection or emotion in his voice. 'He's not dead? He still lives?'

'But — but,' James stuttered.

'Rumors. We only heard rumors that he had been killed. They never found a body.' Chris rubbed his hand over his jaw. 'Why now, after so many years?'

She opened her mouth to speak then closed it again when she caught Chris's eye.

'Well?'

She fidgeted, uncomfortable in knowing that they hadn't worked it out yet. 'It looks like housekeeping, doesn't it? Dutch is tidying up his old life for some reason.' If they were this far behind, she wondered if they'd discussed Turk yet. 'What was Turk's job in your unit?' she asked to deflect Chris's spotlight glare. Unfortunately, the question had the opposite effect.

'He was the supply officer, bookkeeper, and paymaster. A bean counter. Why?'

146

'He was also a published novelist. Men's adventure novels,' James added. 'Turk was always scribbling — ' His eyes grew wide. 'Papers! You said the men in my flat were looking for papers.'

# 9

Chris shot to his feet and began pacing the area behind the sofa, muttering. 'I'm getting too damned old for this . . . losing my edge . . . more farmer than soldier. Why the hell didn't you tell me Turk wrote books?' he fired at James.

James shifted in his seat. 'I thought you knew. Everybody in the unit did.'

'Well, *I* didn't!'

Emily verbally stepped into the fray. 'Surely you three thought of Turk? He visited James first, then you, Chris. Talk to Mei. She said he had a portfolio of papers with him, and he stayed in James's room while he was here. That visit is what I went to the kitchen to ask her about today.'

Chris stopped behind the sofa, planting his fists in the top of its soft back cushions. He lowered his head, shaking it back and forth. James sat up straighter beside her.

Chris looked up, pinning her to the loveseat with his violet glare. 'Do you have anything else you'd like to point out to us, Emily Noble? Anything else you've deduced or pried out of someone that you'd like to share with us?'

She gulped and said, her voice tiny, 'As I'm here on sufferance and not an active player, no.'

'I don't believe you,' Chris ground out. 'Tell me what came into your mind just now.'

'It's nothing. It's silly. It was just something Manoel and I and some of the other guards talked about this morning when we were taking a walk around the outer compound.'

'Taking a walk with my guards? Plural. The guards who were supposed to be on the roof? The guards who don't even speak English? Those guards?' Chris asked tonelessly.

She nodded reluctantly. 'Manoel translated for us.'

'My guards,' Chris repeated.

'Just tell him,' James urged from beside her.

'Well,' she began reluctantly, 'we were discussing video and arcade war games. James made me play them with him when I was little. I haven't played much since Geoff — It's silly, I tell you. It has nothing to do with any of this.' Her face burned as a blush climbed her cheeks.

Chris growled deep in his throat, much as Gato had done earlier.

All at once her words stumbled over themselves in their eagerness to disassociate themselves from her mouth. 'We, um, speculated that if your enemy doesn't care who goes down as long as you three go down, he should hit this place from the air. That's all it was. Silly, like I said.'

Each word fell into the deepening silence like drops of water cascading from the fountain in the courtyard.

'Emily,' James whispered beside her, 'sometimes you frighten me.'

Sami began to laugh, those strange, almost silent convulsions she'd observed once before.

Her eyes were still locked on Chris. 'That is, of course, if he's given up all pretense of making it appear to be accidental death.'

'Arcade games. My guards.' Chris slowly stood upright as James and Sami, now grinning, exchanged looks and nods.

Sami got to his feet, his bulk efficiently blocking Chris's intended path around the sofa.

James grabbed her elbow with his good arm and hauled her to her feet. 'Maybe you'd better have dinner on a tray tonight, Em,' he said, pulling her toward the door.

'Don't call me Em! Why should I eat in my room? I'm starving. Oh.'

She caught a clear glimpse of Chris's face as he advanced toward her around the opposite end of the sofa, determination in every step. His hands clenched and unclenched in time with his steps.

'Maybe you're right,' she said, and James shoved her out the door.

As she hurried along the tile walk, she heard James's voice, overlaid by loud baritone guffaws that could only come from Sami, since Chris wasn't in a laughing mood.

She went straight to her room and locked the door, hoping someone would tell Mei to send her a tray. She was ravenous but didn't dare venture to the kitchen. If Chris found out she'd gone to the kitchen a second time that day, James would never find *her* body.

She decided to spend her time-out finishing her room search. The shelves in the closet and the topmost bookshelves could wait until she had a flashlight and gloves. She didn't know what insect life lived in dark places in a warm country like Brazil, but she was certain she didn't want to find any of it with her bare hands.

Luiz brought her meal. Before he could set down the tray, she asked him for a flashlight. He agreed to find one for her.

'Has the *patrao* calmed down?' she asked. She busied her hands by lifting the plate cover to see what Mei had sent. If Chris had any say in the matter, it would be bread and water.

His liquid brown gaze flicked to the door. She'd swear those luxuriant lashes had grown longer and thicker and darker since she'd last seen him. The cautious look meant Chris's little talk with his staff must have taken place earlier. Another, stronger one was probably in the works for the guards at that moment.

'For a little while only. He sent for Mei. There was much excitement again after that.'

'At least nobody can blame me for making him angry that time.'

Her little smile vanished when he grinned and said, 'But it *was* you. Mei told him something that you didn't tell him. That made him very angry again.'

With Chris glaring at her earlier, she'd failed to mention that Mei was aware of at least two instances when Turk had been someplace he shouldn't have been, in this room. That's probably what had set him off.

'I think he likes you very much, *senhorita*.'

She paused, and closed her mouth, before she answered. 'Luiz, I don't know how it works in Brazil, but usually when a man repeatedly threatens to strangle a woman, it doesn't mean he likes her.'

His handsome features wore a smug smile. 'You and the *patrao* make love. Clear the air.

Everything all right then.'

Her mouth remained open this time for a solid, stupefying thirty seconds after he left.

She spent the rest of the evening making a mess of the room, dreading a knock on the door, and replaying in her head, with video, Luiz's suggestion. When the knock came, she considered looking for a place to hide rather than answer it. She was relieved to see Luiz again, this time with the flashlight she'd requested. James stood behind him, and the night watch door guard, Ricardo, brought up the rear, waving to her over the others' heads. She smiled and waved back, handed Luiz her supper tray, then closed the door on everyone except James.

For openers, he advised her, 'You know, it might be better if you didn't talk at all when you're around Chris.'

'I think you're right. He wasn't this bad at first. Now, he's angry all the time. I'm sorry, James. For some reason I say and do the most outrageous things when I'm around him.'

'I know you've managed to say and do quite a few since I've been here — and before, apparently. Sami explained the hole in the study floor, with relish and in detail. You've livened him up considerably, by the way. Tonight is the first time I've seen or heard him laugh.' He dropped into the chair, closing his eyes and resting his head against its back. For the first time, her brother looked his thirty-three years.

'You're overdoing, James. You should rest more.' She sat down on the foot of the bed.

'It's the tension, not knowing for sure what's going on or what might happen next. And the memories.'

'You can talk to me, you know. This has been a shock for me, too. I thought I knew you, understood you. I realize now how young you were when you were left the responsibility for a sixteen-year-old girl. Is that what made you sign on with Chris?'

'No. And don't blame yourself for messes I've gotten myself into, Emily. Just think about it. How many times did I make you play soldier with me when no one my age was around, not to mention the video and arcade games you told Chris about? A streak of something was always in me. I wanted adventure.' He made a little sound. 'I got it.'

'A warrior lives inside you. I caught a glimpse of him for a moment after we got you home from Barreiras. That was another shock.'

'I also signed on with Chris because after Mom and Dad were killed, I needed money fast. There was insurance but not enough. Death duties were due on the London flat and the cottage in Cornwall. I realized how much you love that cottage, so I couldn't let it go. And the flat was our home. You were a kid, you needed a base, a place to come home to, even if that place was an ocean away.'

'Then it *was* partly because of me.'

'I needed a home as much as you did. You aren't responsible for the decisions I made then or the ones I make now.' His voice was heated.

'You're an engineer, James.' She motioned toward the door. 'Chris is a soldier.'

'Chris is a farmer who wanted adventure. It was *my* choice. One operation, as a civilian attached, and I'd be set. Chris didn't ask why I needed money up front, but he advanced me enough to send you to your godparents in the States, to pay for art school there, and to pay the remaining death duties. When we returned from Africa, he backed me so I could start my own firm. He did all that without even knowing about you, until you turned up here. He's always doing that kind of thing for his friends. And I've paid back every penny.'

This was a side of Chris she'd begun to suspect when she learned about the men he hired to work Abundancia and how he'd taken in Gato and Mei.

'What happened in Africa, James?'

155

He smiled sadly. 'Chris threatened to shoot me in the other arm if I confided in you.'

'Don't worry about it. He'll blame it on me and shoot me instead. He's itching to do it.'

James leaned forward in his chair, resting his forearms on his knees. 'I've always felt that Cheneyville wasn't over, that someone or something would deliver retribution on us. That's why I kept you out of my public and business life, and why I told you to come to Chris if anything happened to me. I hoped he'd keep you safe.'

'He's keeping both of us safe. If you're not ready to talk about this, I won't push you.'

'I need to tell someone, Emily. I'd rather it be you.' James paused and looked beyond her to somewhere she never wanted to go.

'Cheneyville was a small African village in a tiny country that doesn't even exist anymore. The new president had hidden gold bullion there to finance his takeover and it was time to retrieve it. Our job was to move the gold to the new capital city and guard it en route.

'The plan was that after we delivered the gold, we would guard the treasury while the new government stabilized. My job would be to organize the rebuilding of bridges and railroads destroyed in the coup d'etat.

'Chris was in command. His second-in-command was named Van der Zee, from the

Netherlands, 'Dutch' for short. Chris needed more men than he had in his hand-picked unit, so Dutch came in with his own men. He was recommended to Chris by the new president.

'Our small convoy was scheduled to move out of the village at dawn the next day. That night, Dutch double-crossed us for the gold. He executed anyone who wasn't in on it. No survivors was Van der Zee's code. He butchered the men, women, and children of Cheneyville.'

She wasn't aware that she was holding her breath until it came out on a long sigh. 'Oh, James. How did you and the others escape?'

'We were misplaced in the confusion. That afternoon, three of us had gone with Sami, who was called to a nearby village for a medical emergency. Chris was the only one who knew where we were.

'We came back to find a bloody massacre going on. We had our weapons and ammo, thank God. Chris wouldn't let us go anywhere without them. The gold had been divided between two trucks, parked in two different buildings. Chris was dug in with three of our men around the small building where the second truck was parked. Dutch wanted that second truck.

'We deployed and helped fight off Dutch

and his men, some of whom had been friends when we drove away a few hours earlier. Eventually, Dutch and what was left of his crew took off with the first truck. At the end of it, nobody was left in Cheneyville except the men whose names you know . . . and the dead. Chris was more dead than alive at that point, with a bullet close to his heart. Sami told us Chris wouldn't make it.

'Sami's mother and sisters, all the family he had left, lived in Cheneyville and were raped and murdered that night. He kept from going insane by concentrating on Chris. I think he saved him through sheer willpower. He performed surgery on him right there in the field, among the bodies and the blood, while we stood guard and held lights.

'We radioed from the truck for help. The new president sent his bodyguard unit to pick it up. DelGrosso gave Chris blood. Turk arranged military transport and we got the hell out of what was left of Cheneyville. I came here with Chris and Sami to Abundancia. Chris would live or he would die where he had been born.'

She felt tears on her cheeks. She let him go on talking, as much to himself as to her.

'Chris lived, and he was determined to find Van der Zee and bring him to justice. By the time Chris was on his feet again, we heard

158

that the white-haired bastard had been killed in another incident, along with the rest of his men. Chris remained here at Abundancia, and Sami stayed with him. This place was Chris's other life, and it became Sami's. The rest of us went back to our own.'

'What awful burdens all of you carry,' she whispered. 'I'm sorry I couldn't share your grief and guilt at the time. I wondered about the nightmares but you wouldn't talk about them.'

His eyes focused now. On her. 'You have a talent for cutting to the heart of the matter, Emily. Isn't it Zeus who hurls thunderbolts? You're the female version, banging truths about like I've seen Sami practicing throws with that horrific spear that hangs on the *sala* wall.'

'What was done about the massacre? Were any of you held responsible?'

'We each privately gave statements to the United Nations Human Rights Council. Chris wanted to take responsibility because he commanded the unit, but we backed him up one hundred percent. It was clear that Van der Zee and his renegades were totally responsible.

'We weren't officially guilty, but we weren't exactly innocent either because we were a hired peacekeeping force of soldiers. That was, and still is, a very gray area. After that, we all got out of the business.'

By this time, she had her own theory about why Van der Zee, exposed this evening in Abundancia's *sala* as not being dead, was cleaning house now. She didn't bother James with her ideas that night. She hugged him instead and sent him off to bed.

Finding Turk's papers was more important now than ever, if he had left them here, hidden somewhere. She redoubled her efforts. She'd nearly finished the bookcase, and the bathroom was done, when she heard the sound that, besides gunfire, she anticipated with dread. This knock was more of an attack on one edge of the louvered door.

At least she was presentable. She'd changed her skirt for shorts and had taken off the embroidered shirt. The fact that she was grubby, sweaty, and tired just added to this perfect ending to this long day.

She'd be nice to the man who had helped James and her, because he deserved it. 'Who is it?' she asked, as if she didn't know.

'Open the door, Emily,' Chris said in a voice that brooked no argument.

She opened the door. Chris's eyes were wary, he was shirtless, and he was in a hurry. She took in the hairy expanse of bare chest in a glance. He reached for her hand before he even spoke.

'Good. You're still up and dressed. I need your help with Estrela.'

She dug in her bare heels. 'Wait a minute. What kind of help? It's the middle of the night.' They hadn't parted on the best of terms, and she didn't relish going off into the night with him.

He let go of her and put his hands on his hips. 'Estrela's foaling. It's her first and she needs help. Don't tell me you're going to let her suffer because you and I had problems today?'

Her face must have reflected her decision because he reached for her hand again.

'Wait! Shoes. Shoes would be good, don't you think?'

He leaned against the door frame, looking at her legs while she slipped on her sandals. They cut through the library to the terrace and opened the gate into the outer compound. It squeaked and groaned, a homey sound. He didn't let go of her hand at any point. Maybe he thought she'd make a run for it if he did.

'What do you want me to do?' She looked up at him with a puzzled frown as they approached the stable.

'First, bewitch her like you do Diabo every time you visit him. Make her relax. Then I want you to go in to help me turn the foal.'

'Go in? Go in!' Her sandals left skid marks in the dirt.

He didn't break his stride. When he took his next step, she was simply pulled along. 'Your hands and arms are much smaller than mine. I'll tell you what to do.'

'I don't doubt it. Why would you stop now?' She skipped to catch up.

In the snug, screened stable, most of the box stalls were empty. The laboring, lathered mare lay on her side in the straw in one of them. While Emily watched, her whole body tensed with a contraction.

'You can see she's exhausted. She can't go on like this. We have to help her.'

Emily noted the concern in his eyes and nodded her agreement. She knelt at the mare's head and touched the white star-shaped mark above her eyes, the mark from which she got her name. Manoel had told her that *estrela* meant star. The frightened animal rolled her eyes. Emily stroked the muscled, silky neck and softly spoke to her. After a few minutes she sensed the mare's relaxing.

'Keep talking, Emily Noble. Let her hear your voice, but come back here now.'

She scooted back to him then rose onto her knees. 'You want me to put my hand . . . ?'

'Exactly. Soap your right hand and arm to

the shoulder.' He held up a small rope with a noose at one end. 'Hold this in your palm. Find the foal's head then its front feet. Slip the noose over its front hooves and tighten it.'

'You want me to put my hand . . . ?'

He rolled up her T-shirt sleeve then took her right arm and plunged it up to her upper arm into a deep bucket of warm water. He splashed water up to her shoulder, managing to soak her whole right side in the process. He explained the rest of it while he vigorously rubbed a bar of soap up and down her skin from shoulder to fingertips.

'You'll feel pressure if she has a contraction while you're inside. Try to stay away from her pelvic bones or you'll bruise. Okay, take the noose, press your thumb against the tips of your fingers, and slide your hand — '

'I know. You want me to put my hand . . . '

# 10

She closed her eyes and followed his instructions. While he held Estrela's tail out of the way, her hand and arm glided into the slippery warmth of the horse's birth canal. The soft tissue closed around her, grasping and molding itself to her shape.

When her eyes popped open, Chris was watching her. A question hovered on her lips and heat burned her cheeks. 'I've never felt — ' She cleared her throat. 'Interesting sensation. Is this what a man feels when he's, um . . . ?'

She bit her lip when his face went slack with shock. Then he laughed, loudly and long. She couldn't believe she'd just asked him what she'd asked him. And after James had talked to her about watching what she said. Maybe James had the right idea, and she shouldn't speak at all around this man.

'I'm sorry, Chris. I wasn't thinking.'

He wiped his eyes. 'Yes, you were, just not about horses. You were thinking out loud. Ask me again when we're not so busy. Now, tell me about the foal.'

His look was warm and the heat in her face

ratcheted up to scorch. 'I-I feel something — oh, it's a tail.'

'That's the rump and that's the problem. It wants to come out butt first. Go forward along the foal's side.'

'Now it's something small, round, and soft.'

'With any luck, that's the nose. Great. Now get under its chin and follow its neck to its chest then to its front leg.'

'Oh, there's a hoof. And another hoof. This is like putting together a jigsaw puzzle while blindfolded.'

'Loop the noose around them.'

She gasped. 'She's having a contraction. It feels like a blood pressure cuff!'

'Hang on to the hooves. Don't lose them.'

'Oh, God, will I ever be able to draw again with that hand? It hurts!'

He patted her hip. 'You're doing great, Emily. You're a natural at this.'

'This is a one-time thing, Hawk.' His nickname came out of nowhere. 'You don't have any other pregnant mares lurking, I hope.'

His hand, now on his own knee, balled into a fist and his voice was tense. 'Don't ever call me Hawk. Hawk died in Africa.'

'Sorry, but James calls you Hawk some-times.'

'James was *in* Africa.'

'I see. You had to be there. Kind of a good ol' boy thing.'

When the pressure let up, she slipped the noose over the tiny, slippery hooves and tugged it tight. 'Okay, the noose is in place.' She withdrew her arm and tried very hard not to look at it or to think about eating or washing or brushing her teeth with her right hand, ever again.

Chris stood up and braced his feet. His muscles bunched and danced as he pulled on the rope during Estrela's next two contractions. Their efforts were rewarded when a large foal slithered out headfirst onto the straw.

Tears slid down her cheeks while laughter bubbled up in her throat. Emily dashed them away — with her left hand. Using some straw, Chris carefully wiped the sturdy, wet body, while Estrela struggled to her feet. As he urged the foal on its unsteady legs toward its mother's head, he put his cheek against its neck for a moment. A little smile played around his mouth.

'You and Diabo have a son, Estrela,' he said.

She sensed this man would be as gentle with his own baby as he was with Estrela's. What would Chris's son look like, she

166

wondered? Surely that dark hair and those violet eyes would be the dominant genes. And the son would probably be as stubborn and willful as his father.

Chris's right arm came to rest loosely around Emily's waist as they watched Estrela make a nuzzling acquaintance with her colt.

'I've never seen anything being born before.' She whispered out of reverence for what she'd just seen. 'It was beautiful. Thank you for asking me to help you.'

'I've seen it many times, and it still awes me. I want to watch *my* son being born someday.' Then he caught himself. 'I mean, at one time I did.'

She looked up at him in surprise. Did he somehow know what she'd been thinking a few moments ago? Her heart and breath tripped when she saw glowing warmth in his eyes. They were also filled with naked longing.

'We'd better get cleaned up,' she said in a faint voice. 'It's late. Or early.'

Chris let her use the bucket to wash first. There wasn't enough water or soap in the world to make her arm and hand feel clean at that moment. A soaking bath or a long shower or a scrub brush, or all three, might help when she got to her room.

The well-developed muscles in Chris's

arms, back, and shoulders rippled as he took his turn with the bucket and soap. In that instant she didn't want to be alone with this experienced, knowing, and unsettling Brazilian on the long, dark return journey across the outer compound to the terrace gate.

She didn't dwell on whether it was Chris or herself she didn't trust as she slipped out into the night. Her eyes soon adjusted to the fading darkness, and she moved briskly toward the house until a large, warm hand closed over her shoulder. Her potential scream was stillborn in Chris's flood of angry words.

'You don't take orders well, do you? I ordered you never to go anywhere alone.' He swung her around, into his arms, the very arms she'd tried to avoid.

'But I'm not alone, the guards — '

'The guards be damned,' he said gruffly. 'I brought you out here and I'll take you safely back to where I found you.'

When she pushed lightly against his bare chest, her fingers found satin skin and silky hair. So, she tried to twist out of his unyielding grip. That resulted in her breasts beneath her T-shirt being crushed against him when he pulled her even closer.

'You are the most exasperating, fascinating, outrageous woman I've ever met, with the most beautiful legs I've ever seen. I've been fighting this since the night you shot at me in my own study. Your magic works too well, *querida*, with drawings, with horses, with cats. And with me,' he admitted as his lips drew near hers.

'Wait, Chris.' Where had her breath gone?

He stopped, watching her, his own breathing ragged.

'Don't hold me like I'm a sack of soybeans slipping out of your grasp.' When his hold on her eased, she slid her hands up over his chest, reveling in the sensations of hair and skin they found there, before moving up around his neck. 'I've been fighting this, too, but if it's going to happen then let my first kiss be given freely, not taken by force.'

'*Meu Deus*,' he muttered as the tiny gap between them diminished.

In the moment prior to their lips touching, she felt a tingle arc between them, like electricity, before a flurry of sensations overwhelmed it. Bordering on sweet pain, they ricocheted from her lips, to her breasts, to her thighs, to the place where his fingers, under her T-shirt, played across the small of her back. Her senses clamored from the overload.

Her hands moved across the tawny, firm skin of the back of his shoulders and neck in slow caresses while she melted against him, hollow to curve, curve to hollow. His hands answered by moving up her back, making her aware of their progress as she had never been aware of a man's touch before.

Not until his movements against her mouth gentled to feather soft did she open her lips beneath his. She trembled then, and it communicated itself to him, echoing through him and back into her.

He groaned and put her away from him. 'I want nothing from you but pleasure, Emily, yours and mine. You have to understand that. Where there is no commitment and no trust, there is no pain.'

Those words stole her breath in a different way. Had she really thought, just from the power of a single kiss, that she might be different from his other, casual women? She took a deep breath to steady herself and her voice.

'Where there's no commitment and no trust between a man and a woman, there can be no love. I'm an old-fashioned girl about that, Chris. And I make my own mistakes. I don't pay for anybody else's, especially mistakes other women have made with men. I won't — '

A tiny red spot of light appeared in the middle of his forehead. She didn't believe her eyes at first, but she'd watched enough action movies to recognize a locked-in laser sight when she saw one. And she'd seen something very similar just recently, Gato's laser mouse pointer toy.

Those thoughts coincided with her movement. Her fingers still rested lightly on the back of Chris's neck. She dove to the right, pulling him with her. They landed in a heap, with her on top, more or less.

She heard it on their way down, the crack of a high-powered rifle, the sound trailing the bullet that would have blown Chris's head off. He flipped her off him, protecting her with his body. While the warm weight of him pressed the whole length of her body into the dirt, every dip and curve in hers met a corresponding hill or valley in his. Shouts sounded all around them, and the guards on the roof returned fire. He rolled off her.

'Stay low and keep your head down.' He pulled up his pants leg and retrieved a handgun from a leg holster.

He was cool under fire, she'd give him that. The words were said in the same tone he'd use to say, 'Have a nice day.'

They scuttled back to the stable in a low run. He quietly closed the door behind them and pushed her into the nearest stall. She almost panicked, but anger saved her, unreasonable anger that someone almost killed Chris in her arms a moment ago, personal anger that one madman could make her afraid like this, and a deeper anger because man still killed man for reasons that never made sense. She sensed that anger was better in this situation, because Chris would slap her silly if she became hysterical.

'You wanted to know how we'd know he's here. We know. He must be watching the house. I've certainly given him enough opportunity around the farm,' he whispered an inch from her ear.

She gasped. Quietly. 'So that's what you've been up to. Where did the shot come from? Could one of your men be working for him? Feeding him information?'

'Possibly.' His tone let her know he'd already considered it, reluctantly.

'I don't want to think it either, Chris.'

He placed one finger against her lips. 'Be quiet, starting now.'

They heard men's voices. Vehicle engines fired up and roared off into the night. And still they waited. For what, she didn't know — until she heard footsteps outside. He wanted quiet? She gave him quiet. She stopped breathing.

The stall door was open a crack. Chris brought up the gun, supporting it with both hands, and aimed it steady and true at the stable door.

'Emily?' James's voice quavered. 'Emily, please don't be dead.' Her brother's anguished words made her breath catch in a half-sob.

Another voice instantly hushed him. She recognized Sami's soft tones. And still Chris waited. Not until Sami said one phrase in a language she didn't recognize did Chris betray their hiding place with his strange, one-word response. Even then, Sami opened the stable door slowly, coming in gun first, and Chris did the same with the stall door. James came straight to her, enfolding her in a fierce one-armed embrace.

'Are we secure?' Chris's voice was low and cool and all business.

Sami nodded. 'It came from the grain storage silos, we think. A roof guard saw the flash. He'll lose himself in one of the tall fields.'

'Were we set up?' No one could miss the grim note.

Sami shrugged. 'He could have been waiting for morning and took an opportunity shot. Did you talk to anyone except me when you came back to the house to get Emily Noble?'

'Her door guard. Every damn guard on the

roof knew I had been in the stable and that I was going back with Emily.' His gaze flicked her way. 'Luiz was straightening up the *sala*.'

'So late? He's not in the *sala* now and he's not in his room. I was checking the house when I heard the shot.'

'Make sure everyone's accounted for. We'll search the house, top to bottom. Emily's room first. Get a couple of the guards.' He turned to her and James, avoiding her eyes. 'And then I want her in that room, James. Stay with her until I come back. Don't open the door to anyone except me or Sami.'

And that's how it was done, quietly and efficiently and thoroughly. She wasn't too surprised to learn that James was armed, too. Before they slipped out into the sunrise, he self-consciously lifted his pants leg and extracted a gun, much like the one Chris carried, from a leg holster.

'Thanks for helping me retreat, James,' she said as they started back to the house at a low run.

'We never use that word. We're just advancing in a new direction.'

He took her through the *sala* and grabbed a bottle of whiskey from the bar before they went to ground in her room. Locking the bedroom door behind them, he did a quick turn around the room and the adjoining

174

bathroom, made sure all the louvers were closed, turned off the lights, then settled down in her chair. He propped up his stockinged feet on the needlepoint footstool in front of it, with the gun resting in his lap. She rested on the bed on her right side to wait, watching James in the gloom.

'Are you okay?' she asked.

He snickered. 'I've been better. How about you?'

'Same here.'

He stood and passed the bottle to her. 'For medicinal purposes?'

She took a sip, shivered, gasped, then handed it back. He put it on the floor beside his chair.

She didn't mention what she'd heard him say outside the stable door, but silently acknowledged that death had passed her in the darkness that night. It was suddenly very important that her brother know how much he meant to her.

'I love you, James. Be careful in this life.'

'I love you, too, little sister. I didn't realize how much until a little while ago. I'm sorry you were dragged into this. I hoped you were safe, thousands of miles away. I really did e-mail you that I'd be out of touch for a while. Dutch must have intercepted the message.'

'Then it's not your fault that I'm here. And if this man is as ruthless as you say he is, he would have kidnapped me or something, wherever I was, to get to you.'

'Maybe. Try to get some rest.'

She smiled at the far-fetched thought. 'I will if you will.'

She was asleep in ten minutes. Sami's knock on her door sometime later, and James, gun held high in both hands, plastering himself against the wall beside the door, brought her back to wakefulness in a hurry. Her head pounded from the moment she lifted it from the pillow.

'All clear. Details at eleven,' he told her after Sami departed.

'Did they catch him?'

'No, he was long gone. But they found Luiz cowering with one of the worker's daughters in an outbuilding. He says they fell asleep in each other's arms. They thought her father and brothers had arrived with their shotguns when the shooting started.'

She smiled, in spite of her aching head, glad that Luiz was in the clear, with Chris at least. 'I have a terrific headache. I'm going to shower, take a pill, and go back to bed. Unless there's smoke or blood, I don't want to be disturbed. Try to arrange that for me?'

He dropped a kiss on her forehead. 'I'll tell the others and Luiz. Lock the door behind me.'

She ignored Luiz's gentle tapping on her door a few hours later. But when large booted feet stomped up to it ten minutes after that, she realized her mistake in not answering it the first time.

Chris's knock shook the door. 'Sami gave me some tablets for your headache.'

'Thank him, but I've already taken something.' The worst of it was over, but she still cringed as her raised voice shot arrows of pain through her head.

'Open up. I want to talk to you.'

'Go away. Let me die in peace.'

'Unlock this door, Emily, or so help me I'll break it down!' His voice was now ominously quiet.

She checked to see what she was wearing. His T-shirt. Again. She'd bought two nightgowns, hadn't she? She stalked to the door and threw it open, staggering slightly under the intensity of his look. She hadn't seen him since their kiss.

'You are the most aggressive, overbearing, infuriating, annoying man I have ever met! I asked to be left alone. And why would you threaten to break down a door when the spare key hangs in your own kitchen?' She climbed back into bed and turned away from him.

'Because I'm not allowed in my own kitchen and you know it.' He followed her. The bed moved as he sat down on it. 'Did I hurt you last night, er, this morning when I rolled on you?'

That kiss, and what it made her feel for a man who wanted nothing but her body and offered nothing but his, was the most hurtful thing that had happened to her last night, er, this morning.

'You didn't hurt me. This is just a stress headache. I get them sometimes when I don't get enough rest.'

'I can't imagine why you'd get a stress headache here.' When she didn't respond to his humor, he said quietly, 'I want to talk to you about last night.'

'Which part? It went on and on and on. You sure know how to show a girl a good time.'

'I have that reputation.'

She heard the smile in his voice for the second time and turned onto her back so his dimple was in view. 'One of many, I'm sure. What part of last night is up for discussion?'

'The, uh, the kissing part.'

'I thought you might reconsider our rash action in the harsh light of day. It complicates things, and you don't like your relationships with women to be complicated.' She busily folded the top of her sheet over the top of the light blanket. 'I'll make it easy for you. It's okay. Forget it. It never happened.'

He put one hand on each side of her and leaned in, making her go still. 'But it did happen and I can't forget it. In fact, I can scarcely think of anything else. I've never before met a woman I'd like to kick all the way to the airport at Barreiras one minute, and kiss her senseless the next. You'll have to bear with me while I sort myself out.'

She watched him draw closer, a centimeter at a time. 'You're thinking about doing something now that you'll regret later, aren't you?'

'No, I'm thinking of doing something now that we'll *both* regret later.'

She put one hand against his chest then jerked it back when she felt his heart pounding beneath it. 'Look, I'm at a disadvantage here. I'm not fighting fit today, and I'm in my jammies, or rather your T-shirt, my head is threatening to burst — '

'Keeping you at a disadvantage is the only way I can get a word in, or stop you from saying something that makes me angry and distracts me, when the only thing I really want to do is . . . '

She had to do or say something to make him angry and distract him because the only thing she really wanted to do was . . .

She spoke so quickly the words jammed together. 'So, did you make love to her in this bed?'

# 11

He closed his eyes, took a deep breath, and sat up straight. 'Well, *that* little side trip didn't last long. Thank you. It's probably for the best.'

He got up and paced back and forth until she thought she would scream. She carefully sat up and arranged the pillows behind her.

'Stop that!' she snapped. 'Do you have something else to say about last night or is this just general harassment?' She massaged her temples.

He stood at the bottom of the bed, reaching up with his right hand to tug on his ear. 'Shall we just put all this . . . attraction . . . and the kiss down to forced togetherness and an adrenaline high?'

'Let's. And since *I* kissed *you* last night, it was my adrenaline high at work. *You* are responsible for yours. Are we clear on that? Fine. Now, if you'll excuse me. It's hell sleeping in a shrine, isn't it?'

If she could recall the words, she would. The look on his face warned her there would be consequences for one of them. She wasn't sure which one. He slowly walked along the side of the bed toward her.

Her fingers clutched the sheet. 'If you're going to strangle me, make it quick. And quiet. Please.'

'Oh, I will. Understand me, Emily.' He pointed toward the closet. 'Those clothes don't make this room a shrine. Maria is a women's clothing designer. She makes up her samples to her own measurements. Maria of Rio?'

Another piece of the mystery woman's puzzle snapped into place. Maria Pandolfo. Maria of Rio. 'She's a designer with exceptional talent, Chris.'

'And ambition. Those were the problems. She couldn't work from here. She needed to be in Rio, and she needed a man who could be in Rio with her. She found him. She asked me to store the clothes she left behind until she sent for them. That was two years ago. She hasn't and she probably won't. I was going to ask Mei to pack them up and send them to her. All that's left of Maria Pandolfo at Abundancia is in that closet.'

Her little laugh was hollow with disbelief. Couldn't he see that Maria of Rio had left him so damaged that he wouldn't pursue a committed relationship? He sat down on the edge of the bed again. She couldn't look away from those mesmerizing eyes if she wanted to.

'The clothes have served a completely different purpose than the one you imagine. They remind me that it takes a special kind of woman to be happy in the *cerrados*, and that I don't have the time or the masochistic streak necessary to winnow out the ones who can't bear the isolation. As a result, I take my pleasure with no commitments, no trust, and no regrets. Interested?'

She slowly shook her head and gulped down the lump in her throat. 'Sorry, dear, I have a headache.' Her knuckles were white, so she relaxed her grip on the sheet. 'But thanks for asking. I've seen the hurt in your eyes when you look at that closet, Chris. After two years, part of her is still in here somewhere.' She tapped him on the chest. 'And she's certainly in your head, if you've altered your dreams and moral code because of her. Or maybe you always dreamed of being a playboy?

'As for me, I'm a package deal. Geoff wanted my heart and soul and mind, such as it is, as well as my body. And I had saved it all for him. He was my first everything, first love, first fiancé, first and only lover. In that order. I won't settle for less than love from you or from any man.'

'What's love got to do with it?' He moved in, enfolding her in his arms. 'Surely there can be no harm in another kiss, Emily Noble, just to see if our memories serve us correctly?'

His kisses were loaded with harm for her, but she couldn't express that to him. 'A *last* kiss, Christovao of the Cerrados, then we go our separate, not-very-merry ways. And it's your call whether this one is down to an adrenaline high or forced togetherness.'

Like a flower turning toward the sun, she lifted her face for him. His exquisite tenderness melted her resolve as easily as it melted her bones. Their kiss grew deeper and more urgent until they devoured each other. One warm, callused hand was on a mission beneath her T-shirt. In a caress beginning at her hip and approaching the softness of her bare breast, it set off warning bells in her head — and everywhere else. She forced herself to tear her mouth from his.

'*Tigresa!*' he whispered, his breathing ragged.

'*Tigre!*' she said on a gasp. 'Now go away. Lust isn't enough for me. It will *never* be enough.'

He didn't look back and that didn't surprise her. What shocked her was how slowly he walked to the door, like a man in a daze. Or a man who had just faced an awful truth.

She refused to acknowledge why she cried bitterly after he left. Chris could have any woman he wanted. Why did he want her when she needed so much more from him than he was willing to give? No way was *she* falling in love with him. She totally ignored the obnoxious little voice in her head that insisted she had already done so.

Before she entered the *sala* that evening, determined to pretend that nothing had happened between her and Chris, she heard three male voices go suddenly quiet at her foot-steps. Chris's not-so-innocent kisses were almost forgotten, because of the way they looked at her, like someone had pulled her pin and they were counting the seconds until she exploded in their faces. She paused in the doorway, letting the damning silence settle around her like falling leaves. Their conversation had most certainly been about her.

Chris stood up when she stepped farther into the room, and the other two leaped to their feet. James and Chris held drinks. Sami did not.

'Let me get you a sherry.' Chris headed for the bar.

'I don't want anything, thanks.' She looked from one to the other to the other. 'What's happened?'

'Have a drink, Emily.' James didn't often use that tone of voice with her. When he did, she usually did what he asked.

Surprise colored her words while dread colored her thoughts. 'Gee, let me think. I think I'll have a sherry. But I'll drink it standing up, so you might as well sit down.'

She strolled around the *sala*, eyeing all of them but especially James, who now looked anywhere but at her. Sami looked at Chris and at James and at her in turn, a tiny smile on his face.

He finally spoke. 'Chris wants to fill you in on what we found this morning.'

She was glad she wasn't on the receiving end of the look Chris shot Sami before he began. 'The shooter was on top of one of the northern grain storage silos, the ones we passed on our way to Barreiras. They're the closest high ground. We found a brass cartridge and the remains of a meal. We had a man posted there. He's dead.'

She gasped with shock and walked over to stand near James where he sat on the loveseat. 'Oh, no. Do I know him? Was he a family man?'

Chris took a large sip of his drink. 'No, you didn't and he wasn't. My friend Marcos heads the police force in Barreiras. I've reported the incident and the murder to him

186

and gave him an abridged version of what's going on. I'm the law enforcement presence around here, so I have to keep him in the loop now.'

'Dutch killed the man on duty at the grain silos, bided his time until he got you in his sights, and disappeared into the fields when he missed his shot?'

'It looks that way. I've questioned every one of my guards. I haven't changed my mind about any of them.'

'Oh, I'm glad. I like every one of the guards I've met.' She paused. 'So, are you going to tell me the new plan? All this furtiveness shouldn't go to waste.'

When nobody answered, she turned her attention, like a floodlight, on her brother. 'James, you might as well tell me what's going on. I'll have it out of you somehow.'

James muttered a curse under his breath and took a drink of his whiskey. Instead of answering her, he looked at Chris.

'Tell her,' Chris said in soft, icy tones.

'I never wanted this to touch her.' The pain in James's voice brought her a step closer to him.

'It's already touched her.' Heat licked Chris's words. 'With three of us here together, that puts her right in the bastard's sights as long as she stays. Bull's-eye!'

'Stop talking about me like I'm not here,' she said in tones that usually sent James elsewhere.

They ignored her.

James fired a question at Chris. 'How can you be sure it's safe?'

In two steps she was in front of Chris. She clutched his khaki shirtfront in both fists and shook him. Actually, he scarcely moved, but she got his attention. 'Someone tell me what's going on!'

He looked down at her hands. 'I wish you'd fight this need you have to make me look untidy.'

She let go and slowly began smoothing the wrinkled material across his chest with her palms. His nearness and the hard-muscled body beneath her hands sent disturbing little ripples of heat across her skin.

When she realized what she was doing, she murmured, 'Sorry,' took her sherry off the bar, and sat down beside James on the loveseat.

Lifting her chin, she threw back the sherry and plunked down the empty glass on the game table in front of her. 'Okay, I'm sitting down and I've had my calming drink. Believe it or not, I'm a reasonable person. I've been told horrible truths, stupid plans, and bad jokes, and lived. What are you three planning after you dump me somewhere?'

The three male faces each wore a sheepish smile now. Despite the grudging respect in Chris's eyes, and Sami's, she still wanted to slap them on general principles. Instead, she elbowed James, who was closest to her and a relative, out of sheer bad temper. He merely grunted.

Chris sat down on the sofa across from her. 'After we send you somewhere safe, we've decided to offer Dutch a series of opportunities that will make him think we're letting down our guard, or that we're daring him to come after us. Both will make him angry. If he's angry, maybe he'll make a mistake.'

She was struck dumb for a moment. Sadly, it didn't last. 'Maybe he'll make a mistake? I'm glad I won't be here to see this. Let me guess. Open the gates. Give the guards liquor and women and the night off. And bull's-eye T-shirts for everyone?'

A muscle worked in Chris's jaw before he continued. 'We have to do something to end this. He's after *us*. We don't want to put you in danger again. You could have taken that bullet this morning.'

'The laser sight was locked in on *your* forehead, not mine.'

'This time. And only because you didn't move into the line of fire.'

'By the way, did I miss your thanking me for saving your life?'

'No. I forgot. Thank you.'

'You're welcome. Let's do it again sometime.'

James's and Sami's heads swung back and forth, following their exchanges.

'Now, may I finish?' Chris watched her, daring her to speak.

She decided not to risk it.

'With you to protect, we can't concentrate on Dutch. Tomorrow night we'll take you dancing in Barreiras. Sami will set up the security. When we leave Paulo's, we'll create a diversion. In the confusion, we'll slip you into a convent van. The sisters will transport you to their convent located in an upscale suburb of the town. You'll be safe with them.'

'Me in a convent? 'Get thee to a nunnery'?'

James chuckled beside her. 'If they hear how she dances, they'll never take her in. Better tone it down, Em.'

Chris flicked a surprised glance at James then a shocked one at her.

'Don't call me Em. And you're right, they won't.' She'd had some memorable times on the dance floor and couldn't help but smile at the memories. 'I danced with a Brazilian student once. I don't think it was legal.' She noted Chris's glower and returned to

190

business. 'Why are you so sure I'll be safe there? And won't my presence put the nuns in danger, if I'm not?'

'I hope Dutch has lost interest in you as bait. He wanted to use you to flush out your elusive brother. He doesn't have to do that now.' Chris bared his teeth in a semblance of a grin. 'And no man has ever passed those convent portals. I doubt the Pope could get in.'

A general stillness reigned for the ten seconds it took her to surrender to common sense and to the strength of their reasoning.

'Okay, I'll go quietly.' The echoes of her words plummeted into the stunned silence that settled thick and heavy in their midst.

James turned sideways to look at her. 'Just like that? No arguments?'

'I came here, brother, to find you because I was worried about your safety. If you tell me it's time for me to get out of the way so you three can take care of business and end the danger, then it's time for me to do what I'm told.' She glanced over her shoulder. 'I see Luiz is hovering. Is dinner ready? I'm starving.'

James looked at her but his words were meant for the others. 'You'll have to excuse my sister. She has the appetite of a lorry driver. She was strange as a child as well.'

191

Chris held her chair for her, just as he'd held it for her every night they'd eaten together at Abundancia. When he sat down, however, his mouth was set in a thin line and a muscle worked relentlessly in his tanned cheek. Every time he came near her now, she felt a tug, an invisible force pulling her body closer to his. She wondered if he felt it, too. She had crossed her own line when she responded to his kisses. The time had come to get away from this place and this man, before both of them made her reevaluate the rules she loved by. Time to *fugir* by way of a convent.

She was hungry, yet she couldn't wait for dinner, with its last-meal feel, to be over. Her mind skirted around what would happen tomorrow night. These men at the table with her would put themselves in harm's way to take her to safety. Tears threatened when she wondered if all of them would be alive this time tomorrow. Ten days ago her life had been so ordinary. How could it overflow with so many new, amazing feelings and so much fear and danger in such a short period of time?

The sparse conversation was a farce compared with the group's usual banter. She replied when spoken to. Her comments, preoccupied and polite, did their part to keep the flow moving but did nothing to relieve the strained atmosphere. Luiz sensed it. His service was accompanied by furtive glances at Chris and lots of clattering and clanging.

She escaped to her room as soon as she reasonably could, aware that Chris watched her leave the *sala*. She changed her skirt for jeans and set to work. If Turk's portfolio was in her room, she had to find it tonight, or tomorrow at the latest. She wasn't surprised when Chris knocked on her door a short while later.

'Can you use some help?' he asked when she opened it. 'I sent James and Sami to finish up James's room.'

She stood in the doorway, blocking his path. 'Are you sure you want to risk more forced togetherness?'

'I will, if you will. We're adults. I think we can control ourselves.'

She stepped back at his look, making a sweeping motion into the room. 'Come in. You might see something I've missed, if I tell you where I've already looked. I haven't done any high areas yet. I'm finishing up the books and the bookcase.'

With two shelves to go, she sat Indian-style on the floor in front of the bookcase. He pulled the armchair over, stood on the seat cushion without taking off his boots, asked her for the flashlight, and swept its beam across the top of the bookcase.

She stole a look upward at his tight, just right Brazilian butt. Although his clothes were a workingman's fit that he could move in, they were neat and skimmed his body, hinting at the underlying bumps and mounds of well-developed muscle. She fantasized about how much clothing she could get him to remove, if she talked him into posing for her.

He stepped down and turned to the closet. 'I'll do the shelves above. I'll leave the clothes to you.'

From the closet shelves he moved to the mattress and box springs, which she couldn't wrestle alone. Finished with the bookcase, she helped him tear the bed apart. She accepted his offer of help to remake it when they'd finished. They worked well together.

Eventually, she became aware that the cool, smooth sheets and soft blanket were tidy and that they were staring at each other across the bed's width. 'M-Manoel tells me you're clearing more land,' she said into the heavy silence.

'I plan to put in more coffee. Buyers say Western Bahia coffee is the best in Brazil.'

She turned to the nightstand on her side of the bed. He did the same on his. 'Is the land hard to clear? I didn't notice many trees.' In

194

fact before the fields started, all she had seen were low-growing shrubs and stunted trees here and there across the grasslands.

'Even without many trees, it takes a lot of men and backbreaking work to clear one hectare of the *cerrados*.'

'So how do you go about it?' She had emptied the bed stand drawer. Now, she pulled it out and turned it over.

He picked up the flashlight she rolled across the bed to him. 'We attach a cable or chain between two tractors and go over the land a couple of times, in opposite directions, to knock down the vegetation. After that, the woodcutters move in. The larger pieces go to a soybean processing mill for fuel. The brush is burned. We disc in limestone and phosphorus with tractors. Roots and branches are picked out by hand. In February or early March the seedlings go in.'

She slid the drawer back into place and put her few things inside it. 'So coffee is a moneymaker for Abundancia?'

'Yes, and eventually these new fields will make money also. Coffee can be planted on newly opened *cerrados*, but it's a patience crop. We wait eighteen months for the first small harvest. It takes forty-two months for a mature yield harvest, with once-a-year harvests after that.'

James joined them then and she could have hugged him. The two men moved the bureau, the desk, and the dressing table to look behind them and to examine the furniture's backs and undersides. They tackled the back of the bureau after she told them she had done the bureau drawers earlier, when she needed a break from books. She checked behind the framed botanical prints on the walls. They searched the feminine little desk for secret drawers. Chris tilted the wing chair forward and James supported it while Chris looked at its bottom. The room wasn't carpeted. Throw rugs or area rugs had been placed strategically around the tropical hardwood floor. They looked under each for loose floorboards.

'Turk must have taken it with him. Maybe that portfolio has nothing to do with any of this,' Chris said finally.

He could be right. She hadn't mentioned her new idea yet, hoping someone would take the direct route by finding the portfolio and any damning evidence it might hold. She looked away, not wanting to catch Chris's eye.

'Oh, no,' he muttered.

James had seen the look. 'If you have any ideas, Emily, now is the time to share them.'

# 12

'Well . . . Now don't look like that, Chris. Maybe you've already thought of this and dismissed it.'

He sighed heavily. 'We're waiting.'

When she didn't speak immediately, they each took a step toward her. She sat down rather hastily in the wing chair. It wasn't nearly as comfortable as it looked. Large men who wore large boots and stood on its cushion would have that effect on a chair.

'Based on what we know and can guess, Dutch faked his death then used the gold to start a new life.'

Chris shot James a look.

'Yes, James told me. All of it. What if Dutch's new life has led him, or is about to lead him, into the public eye? The survivors of Cheneyville know what he looks like. You said he's vain and wouldn't have surgery to change his appearance. You three should get on the Internet and go through press photos for the past nine months to a year and see if you recognize him in any of them.'

James glanced from her to Chris. 'She has a point.'

'She always has a point. Find Sami and get started. I'll be there in a minute.' Hands on hips, watching her, he didn't move after James left.

She couldn't stand the tension building in the room. 'What?' she finally asked.

'I . . . Nothing. Let me know if you find anything in the clothes. You won't . . . '

'Withhold anything I find? Why would I do that? You three are still in danger.'

'No, I meant don't open it. Just bring it to me.'

'Okay. I'm ready for this to end, Chris.' She hoped he knew she wasn't speaking only about the danger. 'I'll do whatever I have to, including getting out of your way . . . and out of your life.'

He nodded wordlessly and left her.

She continued to sit, squirming, in the chair long after he left. She rested her head against the back and let her gaze wander around the room, trying, unsuccessfully, not to think about Chris.

She wasn't surprised that Maria Pandolfo, coming from the runways and glamour of the fashion industry, couldn't stand the isolation of Abundancia, professionally or personally. As impressive as Barreiras was, Emily was sure it wasn't a center of fashion, and that's where Maria had to be to stay at the top of her profession. Put Chris's need for peace and his dedication to this place up against her talent and ambition and you had the recipe for a love affair's demise.

Despite Chris saying the clothes meant nothing to him, she was certain their presence caused him pain because she'd seen it. And she was also certain that Maria of Rio didn't walk away from their engagement unscathed. Christovao Santos would be hard to leave.

If Chris had chosen a glamorous women's clothing designer to propose to, then a children's book illustrator who worked in bare feet never stood a chance that he would fall in love with her.

They'd looked everywhere, even the bathroom. The clothes were all that was left to search. The closet had lost its dress-up appeal now that she grasped the full story behind its contents. But she might as well get at it, because it had to be done. Somehow she couldn't see a men's adventure novelist and ex-mercenary named Turk digging through women's clothing, looking for a hiding place. *Oh, this stupid chair —*

She froze as she shoved her hand between her thigh and the chair cushion under it. Something was there, under her palm, between the material and the cushion. Impossible. She'd watched them search the chair. James had removed and held the cushion while Chris ran his hands down along the sides and across the bottom of the cushion-less seat. In her mind's eye she saw James feeling over the top of the cushion and squeezing the edges, but he didn't check the underside. If he'd put it back upside down . . .

She removed the cushion from the chair and turned it around in her hands. Maria Pandolfo must have had the chair re-covered because a zipper ran across the back of the cushion. The cover was removable. Shaking now, she unzipped it and cautiously slid her hand inside. Using two fingers, she pulled out Turk's slim, black portfolio, promptly dropping it on the floor at her feet.

She sat down heavily on the chair, sans cushion, before she could bring herself to touch it again. She knew that in a little while she would take the portfolio to Chris, but for this short span of time it was hers. She wanted to know what Turk's papers were about. She'd paid for that right with her peace of mind.

She moved to the bed and unzipped the portfolio. When she flipped open the top, the first thing she saw was a title, 'Collateral Damage: the Cheneyville Papers.' Not a novel, then, as they suspected. And it appeared to be a book proposal rather than a completed manuscript, although some sections were detailed.

Turk had been the paper pusher, and within the pages he'd shown the neat progression of a military operation, in chronological order and in fascinating detail. Besides the manuscript pages, she leafed through copies or originals of supply invoices, transportation schedules, payroll, materiel, munitions, and correspondence between Chris and a man whose name she couldn't pronounce. The letters had traveled into and out of a country that no longer existed. They were very businesslike, from a man who needed a small army to a man who had a small army for hire.

She was a fast reader, and the parts of the book proposal and completed manuscript she skimmed sickened her. Cheneyville was the old story of a rebel president who had to make it on his own and didn't. Cheneyville had finished him, too. And the U.S. had backed this man, though not officially. Her country's government had even recommended Chris's unit to him.

The book ended with the survivors of Chris's unit giving statements to the Human Rights Council of the United Nations. Chris, James, and the other survivors were exonerated, without prejudice. All the men's sworn statements were included, including Turk's, telling of Willem Van der Zee's treachery.

At the back she found pictures. She suspected she would forever regret it if she looked at them, yet how could she not? She soon saw and understood the many reasons for James's nightmares. Tears ran down her cheeks, but they didn't interrupt her rhythm of look, shudder, lay aside, until just one was left.

The last photo was a small group of men, all wearing camouflage. Her heart stuttered when she recognized a younger Chris, with his camouflage shirt-jacket open at the neck and the sleeves rolled up. But the image of the man with white-blond hair who stood beside Chris riveted her to her seat in horror and disbelief. Her breath clogged her throat, her tears ceased, and her blood thumped in her ears as the room spun around her.

He still looked the same. His hair was dyed, of course, to the sandy blond color he now wore. And he must wear colored contacts in the life she knew him in, because in it his eyes were a light blue.

If this man had been one of the men in James's flat, she hadn't recognized those almost colorless eyes or anything else about him. She thought back to that man's size, his build, the way he carried himself, his voice. His disguised voice. With a sickening thud, her conclusions tilted and tumbled into place. Yes, it had been the same man in London who answered to a different name in New York City.

With numbed fingers she shoved everything except that picture into the portfolio and zipped it shut. Now, she would take it to the *sala* or the study or wherever they were and tell them that she knew a monster, too. The same one they knew. She would do all that, right after she located a certain sketch she'd drawn. And right after she threw up.

She found them in Chris's study. She hadn't been in that room since the night she came here. Her eyes sought the marred floor where the bullet she'd fired drove into the wood between Chris's feet.

Intent on the computer screen, they didn't notice her at first. James and Sami sat at the desk. Chris leaned forward behind them. With their new awareness of each other, he soon looked to the side, at her. He slowly stood upright, his eyes on the portfolio. She carried it by one corner, between her thumb and forefinger, not wanting to touch it. Chris had been speaking. When he stopped in mid-sentence, James and Sami looked at her, too.

She saw them with new eyes. Even the proposed UN-approved newer, kinder, gentler mercenary units, specially trained, adhering to a code of ethics, and hired by legal governments for peacekeeping, would still be guns for hire. People would continue to die wherever they went, innocent people sometimes. It would take a lot more time to get her mind around the fact that two men she loved and one she highly respected had been present at this horror she held between two fingers.

'I — I found it ten minutes after you left. The chair was re-covered. The seat cushion has a zipper.' She held out the portfolio, holding it as much away from her as toward Chris.

He saw the look in her eyes and his mouth tightened in resignation. 'You read it.'

'I . . . skimmed it. He included pictures.' Her voice choked off.

'Pictures?' Disbelief was heavy in James's voice. 'Who the hell took pictures and why weren't they entered as evidence when we gave our statements?'

'It had to be Turk,' Chris said. 'He always had an agenda of his own, always legal of course. He must have viewed his being in the middle of a massacre as a golden publishing opportunity.'

The men scanned the pages and fanned out the pictures on Chris's desk. Silence reigned, except when Sami's breath caught. His sound of recognition and pained horror pierced her soul. James's face whitened beneath his tan, giving him a putty color.

Chris glanced up at her, their gazes snagging, before his dropped to the items she still held in one hand. His eyes narrowed. 'Tell us the rest of it, Emily.'

'You'd better sit down for this one, Chris.' She'd kept out the group picture. She held it out to him now, her hand shaking.

Chris took it, reluctantly, his eyes never leaving her face. He glanced at it then handed it to the others. 'That's the least horrific or offensive of any of them. What — ?'

'Is the one you call Dutch the man beside you in the photo?' When he nodded, she swallowed. Hard. 'Then welcome me to the bull's-eye club. I know him.'

They were all on their feet now. Chris spun the leather executive chair until it faced her then he gently but firmly pushed her into it. He stood a few feet in front of her. Sami and James stood on either side of him.

'You know . . . him?' He held the picture out to her.

With a trembling finger she touched the image of the man who stood beside Chris in the photo. 'H-he's my publisher, my boss, William Vanders. He's older now, of course. He dyes his hair a sandy blond and he wears blue-tinted contact lenses. He wasn't wearing them in James's flat. But unless he has a twin brother, that's him in the picture.'

'Willem Van der Zee, William Vanders. *Meu Deus*,' Chris said quietly.

James groaned but Sami made no sound.

'Are you sure, Em?'

'Don't call me Em!' She handed Chris the sketch she'd done of William Vanders. 'Look at the date on this sketch, almost a week ago. It was one of the first I did right out there in your courtyard. You tell me. Is it the same man?'

She continued when the sketch met with stunned silence. 'I've studied that face because he has good bones. He's a millionaire many times over. We've always wondered among ourselves how he made his fortune. Now I know. He owns Tot's Press, among many, many other interests, probably as a tax write-off. He's getting deeper and deeper into politics in New York. I've heard talk of him running for state office.'

'That's his reason for cleaning house now. We know the bastard's face,' Chris said, almost to himself. 'You were right again, Emily.'

She gulped. 'It's no fun being right anymore. I'm giving it up.'

'What else can you tell us?' Chris's eyes held both pain and sympathy but the hunter was very much at home, peering out at her from behind the other emotions.

'The Tot's Press authors and illustrators have two e-mail lists. William — *He's* on the chatty announcement list. About six or seven weeks ago, he posted that he was taking a couple of months off. When I e-mailed him about it privately, he said — he said — '

'We need all of it, Emily.' Chris's voice was even and strong.

'He said he was going h-hunting.'

'*Bastardo!*' Chris spat. Then he put one hand on each arm of his executive chair, but he didn't lean in. 'You e-mail this creep privately. You draw his face from memory. Buddies, are you? Is there anything else we should know?'

She sat up straighter and farther back in the chair. 'James is named as one of my emergency contacts and my sole beneficiary on all my paperwork at Tot's Press. William had access to those records.

'And when James visited me last time, we went into the city and I gave him a tour of

Tot's Press. William was eager to meet him. He was taking us to lunch. I'd glimpsed William earlier, but when James and I got to his office, his secretary told us he'd been called out of town on urgent business.'

'He probably caught sight of James. That must have been a nasty shock. Maybe that's what set off this whole chain of events.' Chris continued daring her with his eyes. 'Anything else?'

'W-William doesn't wear the ring in New York,' she offered.

Chris's gaze never wavered.

'If-if Turk had sold the book or was shopping around that proposal for it, William would have been in a position to hear about it. He knew all the publishing world players. Editors, agents.'

She'd swear Chris's eyes were burning a hole right through her.

'He, uh, William took a couple of his authors and illustrators to Broadway shows, once or twice.'

Chris blinked.

'Emily!' James accused.

Chris pulled his hands off the chair arms like his fingers had been glued down. He turned away to pace the room.

James took his place. 'Emily Tally Noble, how could you?'

'How could I? When your witty, handsome, intelligent boss asks you to be one of a party for a Broadway show opening for which tickets can't be had, most women say yes. He doesn't wear a sign, you know, saying, 'I'm an evil monster.' I didn't know he was nuts.'

Chris's voice came from across the room. 'Evil and pretty and psychotic as hell. Did he ever ask you out alone?'

She tore her angry gaze away from her brother's. 'Yes, many times, but I always turned him down. I don't think it's a good idea to date the boss. That's when he started the group evenings. He said he wanted to show me that he didn't b-bite. But I couldn't really . . . there was something about him . . . when he touched me . . . ' She shivered.

Chris pushed James out of the way. 'He touched you?'

'My arm. He gave me his arm then put his hand on the small of my back when he ushered me to my seat. And he k-kissed me once. His lips were like ice.' She shuddered but recovered quickly. 'What's the matter with you people? This maniac might appear at any moment, oozing Uzis, and you're asking me about my love life?'

Chris turned away from her to speak to James and Sami, literally turning his back on her. 'She's right. Focus. From what he said in

209

James's flat, he wants her, and he probably doesn't know she's identified him in his new life. That might keep her safe for a while. Maybe he plans to console her after we're dead. We'll stick to our original plan. Hide her at the convent until we can get her out of the country and take him out when he comes after us.'

She couldn't believe he still insisted on sending her away and suspected it was equally for her safety and for clearing the field of battle. 'But I'm afraid. What if he — '

Chris was pacing again. 'We'll stick to the original plan.' The voice of a stranger who would brook no argument came out of Chris's full, beautiful mouth.

'All right, I'll go to the convent.' And was that empty husk of a voice hers? 'I'll need something to put my clothes in.'

'I'll loan you a soft-sided weekender. Come to the *sala* tomorrow night at eight.' He glanced at his watch. 'Or rather tonight. Stay in your room until then.' Chris's cool words sent another chill crawling over her. 'Go no farther than the covered walkway outside your room for exercise. We have a lot to arrange before then.'

She was dismissed, in every sense of the word.

Luiz brought her meals on trays, beginning

with breakfast later that morning. She used the surplus of time to read, draw, and pack, then unpack, repack, and play with Gato. She couldn't fit all her things into the case, so she had to be selective. She made room for her drawings of Chris and James.

After she and Gato took a lengthy nap, she allowed herself plenty of time to get ready for the evening. If she never saw Chris or James again, for whatever reason, she wanted them to remember her looking and behaving her best.

She took pains with her makeup and brushed her hair until it shone. She swept up the sides onto the back of her head and held them with a set of silver-edged, black organdy hair combs she'd found while searching the bureau drawers for Turk's portfolio. Wispy tendrils framed her face and the rest cascaded down her back.

In the same bureau drawer she'd also found real silk pantyhose that must have been too long for Maria of Rio, and, shoved to the back of a different drawer, a silver jewelry set, consisting of filigree dangle earrings with a matching necklace and bracelet. The two simple rings she habitually wore had been her mother's. By chance, they were platinum and matched the silver closely enough to look like they belonged to the set.

When she pulled out the lovely black cocktail dress, she discovered a black velvet wrap a few hangers away, and a tiny velvet evening purse that dangled off the same hanger. The wrap would serve to drape over her shoulders and cover her cleavage on the long drive into Barreiras. The high-heeled evening shoes were still a tight fit. If she wasn't whisked away immediately and actually had a chance to dance, she might kick them off. From the remains of her carry-on bag she retrieved the ever-present, tiny bottle of her favorite scent, Tova. She dabbed some on her pulse points and checked her appearance one last time.

Reflected in the mirror behind her, patiently awaiting their regular evening play session, sat Gato. She almost cried when she saw him.

She picked up his laser mouse toy on its key ring, which was in its usual place on the bathroom sink. Tonight, it had been jumbled together with her perfume and her mirrored lipstick case. Gato promptly jumped into the bathtub, his favorite place to play Chase the Dot. She'd discovered while playing with him in their first days together that he enjoyed the moving red dot much more than he did the large red outline of the mouse. So she had unscrewed the tip for him.

Now, she played the pointer dot, ignoring its resemblance to a laser sight, along the sides of the tub and over the walls around it, laughing aloud as Gato stalked, patted, and threw himself upon the elusive dot. Despite his age, he was kitten-like when he played. She would sorely miss her furry little friend, and she was sure he'd miss her. For one wild moment, she considered taking him with her to the convent.

Instead, she gave him a head bump and an extra stroke, swept her articles off the sink into the tiny evening bag, gathered up her wrap, and left her room at Abundancia, and her borrowed cat, probably for the last time. She didn't close the bedroom door completely, leaving a crack so Gato could get out.

She studied Chris and James from the shadows outside the *sala*'s doors for a moment before she stepped into the light. She hadn't seen either of them since the revelations in the study. Chris wore a white, tropical-weight dinner jacket that broadened his shoulders, deepened his complexion, and contrasted wonderfully with his dark hair. He looked good enough to eat. Her handsome brother had made do, to advantage, with a tan safari jacket and matching slacks borrowed from Chris.

Time and the world stopped when Chris's

gaze found her where she stood quietly. James went still, too, once he caught sight of her. He was the first to speak, breaking the illusion that the world stood still.

'You look smashing, love,' he said. He came to her, taking her hands and pulling her into the room. He dropped a kiss on her cheek and looked expectantly at Chris, waiting for an appropriate response.

Chris's gaze swept her from the top of her fair head, to the black high heels on her feet, and back again, pausing on her legs and where the dress exposed the soft inner curves of her breasts.

'Every man in Paulo's will want you in his arms.' His voice was soft and hoarse. 'Shall we go?'

'No. Please, not yet.' Her voice shook. 'I'd like a sherry first. For my nerves.'

Chris ran a finger between his shirt collar and his neck before he poured one for each of them. He raised his glass in a toast. 'To beautiful women, good music, and a successful operation.'

'And God's protection on us,' she murmured before she lifted the glass to her lips, wondering what this night would bring to them.

# 13

Three trucks waited, with the Land Rover sandwiched between the second and third, in the compound behind the house. The men who would accompany them lounged bonelessly against the vehicles, until they saw her. Those wearing hats removed them and held them over their hearts in a salute. Then they all applauded, whistled, and cheered. In the spirit of the compliment, she curtsied gracefully and used both hands to blow kisses to them. Chris allowed her and the guards their moment, then a hand signal from him sent the men scattering to their vehicles.

The largest truck, in the point position at the front, now sported a high cap over the bed. James's truck came next, with a guard sitting beside him. In the snug third position, Manoel chauffeured her in the Land Rover. Manoel, a reassuring presence at her side, was unusually bulky in his casual clothes, obviously well-armed yet with no visible weapons. She assumed the other casually dressed men riding inside the largest truck were also fully armed. Chris, with another man riding shotgun, in a literal sense, held the drag position at the rear.

The ride was rough and long. The road hadn't improved since her first or second trips over it. The worst of the potholes still had tree limbs stuck upright in them. As they weaved around them, she thought their little convoy must surely resemble a caterpillar.

At last the lead truck swung into the parking lot of a nondescript, one-story cement block building on a quiet Barreiras side street. A discreet neon sign announced it as Paulo's. Manoel backed the Land Rover into a space against the building. James and Chris did the same. The lead truck disappeared around the side of the building. Manoel and the two guards stayed with their vehicles.

She felt the thump of the music as soon as James handed her out of the vehicle. Chris walked directly in front of her to the door, and James walked close behind her. The huge man who blocked the doorway looked to be more of a bodybuilder and a bouncer than a doorman. He stepped aside and waved them ahead when Chris greeted him by name and asked after his family. Chris offered her his arm and ushered her into the melee.

Inside, surrounded by walls of sound, tables of men watched tables of women, mixed couples watched each other, and

216

groups of young people watched everyone. All of them paused to assess the new arrivals. The music didn't stop, but all activity other than the wildly suggestive gyrations on the dance floor halted momentarily. She was aware that they presented a striking picture, with Chris's dark good looks against his white jacket, her own fairness in contrast with the black dress, and James's handsome, casual elegance.

Paulo himself came to greet them effusively in English. Chris had a quiet word with him and a table in an alcove near the back instantly became available.

Paulo supervised. 'It is to your liking, *senhor?*'

'*Sim*, Paulo. *Muito obrigado.* The lady likes to dance. Will you spread the word?' he said while setting out his cigarillos and lighter on the dark tablecloth.

'Gladly, *senhor*. The beautiful *senhorita* graces my humble establishment with her presence.'

He intended to go on, probably at length, but Chris smiled, thanked him again, shook his hand, and beckoned the waiter hovering behind the plump owner.

'Why did you tell him to pass the word?' she asked after they ordered. 'I can get my own dance partners, thank you.'

Chris simply smiled around the cigarillo he

was lighting. She wondered what he'd do if she followed her urge to reach out and snap the small cigar in half. He smoked far too much anyway.

'Because no one would ask you to dance unless Chris signed off, so to speak,' James explained for him, his eyes sweeping the tables around theirs. He grinned at a dark-eyed, dark-haired beauty nearby. She grinned back.

'I see. You're the alpha male in the area, and I'm yours by association. And you aren't dancing tonight?' she asked Chris. She let her wrap drift off her smooth shoulders without a qualm, once she'd noted the brevity, top and bottom, of some of the women's clothing.

'Maybe one dance with you, later. I'm on duty.' He had taken the chair that put his back against the wall, while he faced the room.

'Thank you for reminding me. I'd almost managed to forget for a moment. What time will I . . . ?'

'Not for a while. Enjoy yourself.'

She watched the dancers and their movements more closely for several minutes, feeling her jaw go slack. 'The, uh, clothing and dancing are certainly . . . uninhibited.'

'In Brazil, we celebrate the body and its beauty. The more body you show, the better.

Our climate is hot, and our blood is hotter. Both are reflected in our culture, in our dances, and in our sensuality. Here comes the bravest of the lot. Feel free to say no to anyone you don't wish to dance with.'

After the man dutifully greeted Chris and James, Chris introduced him to her. She readily accepted his invitation to dance. He turned out to be the self-confident, handsome manager from another *cerrados* farm. The fact that he spoke English was the bow on a delightful brown-eyed package.

Just as she gave him her hand, the music changed and he hesitated, his soulful eyes troubled. 'It is a lambada, *senhorita*.' He glanced at Chris uneasily. 'Many women who are not of Latin blood will not dance the lambada.'

If Chris wanted her to have fun, then by God, she was going to have fun, and he could watch. She ignored Chris and sent the young man her warmest smile.

'I must have a drop of Latin blood in here somewhere, Felippe, because I'm eager for you to teach me the lambada.' She managed a slow, throaty purr on her next words, despite Chris's glowering frown looming in her peripheral vision. 'Let's find that tiny drop together, shall we?'

Chris achieved, on his own, what she'd

wanted to do a few minutes before. He bit off his cigarillo, deftly catching the lit end before it hit the table or his lap. He spat out what was left, along with a word directed at the young man who led her away. It sounded like a warning.

She immediately responded to the beat and rhythm of this Latin music to her very core, already moving subtly while she walked to the dance floor. Felippe was an accomplished dancer, and she'd been told many times, including by the Brazilian student she'd danced with, that she was a natural. She gave herself up to his tutelage and to the fast beat, rhythm, and primal force of the music surrounding them.

The sexy lambada of this region, a kind of Latin swing, was performed in close bodily contact, thigh-to-thigh, pelvis-to-pelvis, and knee-to-knee, accompanied by rotating hip movements, dips, and swirls. The tempo was fast-paced, yet the steps were graceful. Felippe kept some distance between them, but not much. Most couples weren't as circumspect.

Lines of men, young and old, formed to dance with her after that, each of them keeping a little buffer of distance between her body and theirs, in deference to Chris's watchful attention from the sidelines. She glimpsed James beside her in the throng, bumping and writhing to the beat with the woman he'd smiled at earlier. An hour later she called a halt and returned to their table. James was still on the dance floor.

Chris watched her through the curtain of smoke in the room as she kicked off her shoes and collapsed into her chair. 'There will be trouble. You have the young bucks' blood up.'

'All the easier to slip me into the nuns' tender care. Isn't that the purpose of this outing? Heaven forbid *you* should have any fun.' She sat back and took a sip of her soft drink. 'The lam-ba-da.' She broke the word into syllables, savoring each bit. 'I like it.'

'I could tell. You're very good at it, for a *gringa*.'

'It's . . . primitive, primal.'

'Very. The rhythm originated in the Amazon. The Bahians adopted it and created the movements.'

She sat forward in her chair, elbows on the table, and looked him in the eye. 'May I say two things to you before I'm misplaced in the ruckus and carried off into the night?'

His eyes widened in feigned shock. 'You're asking me if you may speak? What a delightful concept. Thank you for allowing me to believe, even briefly, that I have some control over you.'

'Will you listen or not? James said you helped him, loaned him money for me, when you didn't even know I existed. Thank you for that.'

He lifted one shoulder in a casual shrug. 'You're welcome. And he paid me back. Every dollar, plus interest.'

'I never doubted it.'

'And the second thing you want to say?' He watched her closely.

Sudden stillness descended around them in the chaos and Emily feared she would lose herself in the depths of his violet eyes. In the warm Brazilian night, she sensed the trio of burdens he carried within him. Sadness, sorrow, and regret. He must have felt something, too, because he tilted his head, as if straining to hear. On the fragile tie that bound their senses at that moment, she offered him sanctuary, refuge, peace. Within her heart and within herself.

Just as quickly, the moment passed, but with its passing she realized they didn't need to raise their voices to hear each other, although the music still pumped and throbbed around them.

'Look out for James for me. Please?' Her voice caught on the edges of the words.

His eyes narrowed and a crooked little smile, which she discovered directly affected

222

her ability to breathe, appeared on his tawny, even-featured face. 'It doesn't matter if James comes back alone, as long as James comes back?'

She twisted her glass around, expanding the wet ring on the coaster. 'Surely you know that isn't what I meant. I'll take it very badly if you don't come back together, all three of you. You and Sami are a part of me now.'

'Very prettily and politically said. We'll do our best to look out for each other, as we did once before.'

'Thank you. You know, I'm having a hard time associating the man I know in New York City with the monster who ordered the horrific things I saw in those pictures. Are you going to kill Dutch, or William Vanders, as I know him?'

'Only if he leaves me no choice. And don't forget that he killed the others and that he's trying to kill us. If I can take him alive, I will. Three witnesses are still alive, at this point, and willing to testify against him. I'd like to see him pay for what he did.'

The music changed abruptly to a slow, sexy rhythm. In one fluid motion, worthy of a professional dancer, he pushed back his chair and stood up. 'I've been waiting for this. Will you dance the bossa nova with me now?'

Two groups of butterflies slammed into

each other in her stomach while she slipped on her shoes. One group represented Chris's invitation to dance and all that it entailed. The other took wing because the invitation meant the time was drawing near when she would leave him and James. She dreaded being confined with strangers, even benevolent strangers, and not knowing what was happening at Abundancia.

Chris took her hand and led her onto the dance floor. They passed James, alone, weaving his way between the tables to theirs. She watched the men exchange glances and little nods and had no doubt what it meant.

He gathered her to him, and they moved together to the very slow, samba-like rhythm, hips swaying. She held her own during the elegant and flowing dance, picking up the steps and movements quickly. She felt she gave as good as she got, with interest.

Then the music slid into a lambada. Chris pulled back, looked down at her with a little half-smile, and began to move his hips against her in a way no man should be allowed to move in public without being arrested. His eyes beckoned her even closer, and her traitorous body responded to their unspoken invitation. No buffer of distance, no safety zone, restricted her dance partner this time. Nothing came between them except their clothes and their views on love as they bucked and shimmied against each other.

He let go of her to raise his arms above his head, revealing his watch on one wrist and a gold bracelet on the other. She mimicked his movements then improvised, slowly circling him.

Barely touching him, she drew an invisible circle around his body with the feather light touch of her breasts and fingertips, until she was in front of him again. He brought his arms down to pull her close. Meeting his eyes when she looked up was like crashing into a purple wall at ninety miles an hour.

The music stopped abruptly on a deafening, sour note, when a fight broke out in front of the band. Whether this was the planned diversion or not, it was very effective. Pandemonium reigned.

Chris took a shuddering breath and broke eye contact. Quickly assessing the situation, he grabbed her by the elbow and hustled her back to the table where James sat, watching them and waiting.

'Is there something I should know?' James asked her, looking from one to the other.

'Not that I can think of,' she replied, grabbing her evening bag. 'Unless you're still fuzzy on that Santa Claus versus Father Christmas thing.'

Chris ushered them into the dark, narrow hall leading to the rest rooms. Behind them women screamed, chairs flew through the air, and musical instruments played notes God never intended. He had snatched her wrap off the back of her chair and now draped it over her head.

'Keep your hair covered. It almost glows in the dark. James, go on ahead to alert the men and check things out. I want a word with Emily.'

'I know what you're going to say,' she said, as she watched her brother close the back door of Paulo's behind him. 'Don't horrify the nuns. If anything happens, hit the dirt and stay down until someone comes to me. And hope it's one of you three or one of our men. Oh, and keep my powder dry?'

'Very good,' he said, his voice thin and low. 'Actually, this is what I want to say.'

He slid the wrap off her head, pulled it tightly around her shoulders, pinning her arms against her sides, and backed her into what had to be the darkest corner in Paulo's as he did so.

Her mind registered both fear and fever. 'What are you doing?'

She soon found out, when his mouth came down on hers with sweetly punishing force. The only parts of him that touched her were his lips and his two fists wound tightly in the black wrap against her breasts, yet she was moved as she had never been moved before by a man's touch.

He ravaged her mouth, from a rough taking to a whisper soft tenderness and back again . . . and again . . . until her knees trembled and threatened to give way. Her emotions followed where he led, zinging from a need for tears to wanting to throw him down and lick off his cologne. And then it started all over again. Somewhere along the wild emotional ride, she realized *this* was his last kiss — and he was making it memorable, for both of them.

He finally broke away, his breathing heavy, and stepped back, once again covering her hair with the evening wrap. 'Take *that* to the convent with you.'

Speechless and very nearly panting, she fell back against the wall with a thump, knowing that if she lived to be ninety, she would still carry the searing mark of that kiss on her soul.

'At last,' he murmured. 'A way to shut you up.'

James waited outside the door. 'Not very talkative, are they?' He indicated the white van and the two white-robed nuns sitting in the front seats.

'They're not meant to entertain her.' Chris still held her arm in a loose grip as he guided her toward the vehicle. She broke away to enclose James in a farewell hug.

Still brimming with emotion, she said what came to her: 'Have a care, brother. I want to bounce my nieces and nephews on my knee.'

'Same here, but I somehow think I'm closer to bouncing *my* nieces and nephews.' He shot a sly glance at Chris then touched her on the chin with one knuckle. 'Don't upset the nuns. If they're a silent order, you'll burst.'

From the parking lot out front came the sounds of many engines starting up and tires squealing off into the night. All of Abundancia's vehicles were now parked behind the building. No weapons were in sight, but she was aware that the guns outnumbered the men who moved around them with such purposeful nonchalance. Each had a dark cigarette between his fingers, a broad smile on his face, hearty words on his lips, and restless eyes that never stopped scanning the area.

She pulled away from James with a teary smile and went to Sami, who must have been in the truck with the cap and who now stood at the back of the van. He smiled at her, but she still hesitated to take liberties. She held out her hand to him. He looked at it in surprise then back at her face before he grasped it.

'Look out for them and for yourself,' she whispered, squeezing his hand.

He nodded and she turned to the van. Chris opened the sliding side door and she climbed inside. His borrowed weekender sat on the seat beside her.

'We'll be in touch,' he said in a tight voice and closed the door before she could reply.

He said something in Portuguese through the open window. The nun who was driving started the engine and the van jerked forward.

She coughed at the cigarette smoke drifting in through the nuns' open side windows. Turning, she looked down the length of the van and out the back window. Figures piled into the trucks and the Land Rover in Paulo's back lot. The engines started; headlights flicked on. Three of the vehicles pulled out into the street, going in the opposite direction. She watched one pickup hold back until it was almost out of her sight then it turned and drove the other way.

She'd never felt so alone in her life. If she didn't distract herself in some way, she would soon sob, like a heartbroken, abandoned baby.

'What are your names?' she asked the nuns.

The large nun in the passenger seat shrugged, answering in a pleasantly husky voice. '*No ingles, senhorita.*'

'And I don't speak Portuguese,' Emily said. 'Does it matter? I have to talk or I'll start to cry. And that would be worse, wouldn't it? If I start I might never stop. You don't want to risk that, do you?'

The first nun shrugged again, busily rolling up the window as rain bucketed down on them without warning. Apparently, the *vecancio*, the mini-drought, was over. That would please Chris and his workers, although it would complicate their drive home. She caught her mistake. Their drive to Abundancia.

She talked for miles and miles. She told them about her work and Cornwall and her parents and her motley crew of friends, military and otherwise, on two continents. The driving nun snickered once, so she must have understood something Emily said. When Emily next took note of her surroundings, they were well out of the city, among fields of lush growth as far as she could see.

That gave her pause. Chris had said the convent was in the suburbs of Barreiras, as was Paulo's. They should be there by now, even if it was on the other side of the city. As

230

she thought it, they turned onto a canyon of a road enclosed on both sides by tall, healthy plants. She opened her mouth to ask where they were but instead studied the two broad-shouldered nuns and the inside of the van more closely. A packet of cigarettes, the cheap, workers' brand, and a lighter lay on the floor between the bucket seats. It was smoke from that brand that lingered in the closed van, the dark cigarettes that many of Chris's guards smoked, the brand whose name she could read on the package.

Something was wrong here. She sensed it, felt it. This was the same feeling she'd had in James's flat, before William and his friend grabbed her. Perspiration broke out on her upper lip, making it itch. Her heart did the lambada against her ribs while fear crawled hand-over-hand up her backbone then tiptoed across her shoulders. It wouldn't do to go suddenly quiet. She started to hum a show tune from a Broadway musical she'd seen with William.

It's okay, she silently reasoned with herself. It must be okay. Chris had told her the nuns were an order of social workers. Maybe they had been on a mission earlier in the evening. Maybe the cigarettes belonged to someone they had helped. Or maybe they belonged to the convent handyman or handywoman who might drive the van on occasion. Or . . . not.

In preparation for what might come, she quietly slipped off her high-heeled shoes and found the lever Chris had pushed down to lock the sliding door when he closed it. She switched to another tune from the same show, inching across the seat to the very edge, putting her closer to the door. This road was relatively good and the van moved over it at a brisk pace. She'd break her neck if she jumped out before they slowed down.

She saw no alternative to running into one of the fields. Besides Chris's warning about the dangers of tall fields, the guards had told her many stories about workers or workers' children who had gotten lost in them. William had used one himself as an escape route the night he'd shot at Chris.

If she were wrong about what was going on here, it wouldn't matter if she broke her neck in the jump. Because Chris would break it for her if these were legitimate nuns and she, after all the trouble he had gone to, ran away from them. Into the night. Into the maze that was a tall field.

The roads between large unirrigated fields usually ran very straight. The next road was a gift. It had curves to accommodate the smaller, round fields served by pivot irrigation systems, so the van slowed a little. She put her finger under the sliding door's lock lever. The vehicle slowed even more as it made a turn on a blind curve onto another straight farm road, only to be confronted by the pink-red glow of flares breaking the darkness in their path. Four ways flashed on a bulky farm truck pulled off to the side of the narrow road, almost blocking it. The driving nun slammed on the brakes.

Emily had been happy to discover that vehicles in Brazil were the same as in the States. So, with the driver's side on the left, the big, grumpy nun in the passenger seat in front of her reached up to steady herself with her right hand on the handle above the door. She pulled herself upright as she did so, making her suddenly very tall for a woman.

A ring graced the nun's hand. With a sickening jolt, Emily recognized its green jade stone with a Chinese figure overlaid in gold. Before the van stopped rocking, she pushed up on the lever, flung open the door beside her, and rolled out, straight into a ditch filled with icy water.

# 14

Without missing a beat, she hauled herself out of the ditch and crawled into the greenery, gaining her feet at the expense of her silk hose.

Whatever grew in this field was nice and high. Corn, she suspected. She was glad it wasn't on a pivot irrigation system. Its rows were straight, not concentric circles. She pushed through the growth, both arms extended in front of her, broad leaves slapping her as she passed.

The sounds behind her verified that she had not been riding with nuns from a social order, or nuns of any ilk. Shouted Anglo-Saxon curses and others, more persistent and in a variety of languages, nipped at her heels through the green jungle.

The men in the farm truck called out in amazement and booming gunshots answered them. Then silence descended, except for a steady wind and a now-misty rain that chased each other, whispering, through the leaves. The sound barely covered the racket she made pushing her way through the foliage.

She forced herself to concentrate. By

running in the space between rows then cutting into the next row every few feet, she found she could move along at a brisk pace while moving on a diagonal path deeper into the field. If she kept low where fewer leaves grew, she made less noise.

Her pursuers apparently didn't care how much noise they made, although she eventually heard one call out quietly to the other to stop. She forced herself to stop, too, until her pursuers grew tired of listening and began to move again. The sounds behind her were fainter now.

She put on more speed — until she stepped into a rut, twisted her ankle, and fell heavily. William, or Dutch, the one with any number of names she'd love to call him at the moment, heard her cry out in pain. She stifled a whimper beneath the swish and crunch of his crashing approach.

He recited a litany of curses as he swept aside leaves and trampled plants on his march toward where he thought her voice had come from. For variety, he began a laundry list of tortures he would perform on James King and Christovao Santos. He assured her that they would welcome death before he finished with them.

She almost gibbered with terror as the voice drew nearer. She thought of Chris and that steadied her a bit. Hit the dirt and stay low, he had said. She'd already done that, in spades. She also recalled his voice in Paulo's back hail, telling her to keep her hair covered. Under cover of the whispering wind, she unwound her wrap that was now tight around her neck, curled up into a ball on her side, and pulled the length of the black velvet material over her exposed legs, arms, and hair, any of which might show in the darkness. And she prayed.

He plowed past her a couple of rows over. His boots, showing dark beneath his white habit, were only a few feet from her head. She held her breath, her teeth digging into her lower lip as she fought the scream and panic that threatened to spill out of her. At the moment he passed where she'd gone to earth, she heard every leaf moving, felt every collected raindrop showering down upon her, and wondered if these were the last remotely pleasant sounds and feelings she would hear and feel in this life.

The thin veneer of civilization had burned off the raging man who hunted her. The animal whose fading snarls now moved beyond where she lay had worn a tuxedo the last time she'd seen him. He'd asked her out for the sixth time that night, telling her that he didn't give up easily on anything he wanted. And she'd almost accepted his invitation for a date. Almost.

Too soon after William passed her hiding place, the plants around her were still except for the wind and soft rain. She felt his presence. His waiting. His listening. What if he turned around and searched this small area row by row? *Don't think like a victim*, she cautioned herself, because Chris had told her not to think that way. If he were in this rut, he'd probably analyze what had happened to him and see if he could turn any of it to his advantage, or he'd at least come up with an estimate of when help might arrive. She would do the same to pass the time and to maintain her tenuous grasp on sanity.

Okay. William and Company had stolen the convent's van and two habits. So, how long would it be before the nuns reported the theft? Not long, since they had to be at Paulo's at a certain hour. The police and, she hoped, Chris, would know by now that the van had been stolen. Full stop for that scenario.

If William had hijacked the van, then she hoped the real nuns were safe and had gotten their habit-less selves to a telephone quickly. *No survivors was Van der Zee's code. Don't think like that*, she ordered herself. Again, Chris should know by now that something had gone wrong.

Now, if the convent van, the nuns assigned to this task, and Christovao Santos's friend, one Emily Noble, didn't return to the convent in a reasonable amount of time, surely the nuns would call Chris, and again he would know she was missing by now.

And if all else failed, would Chris call the nuns to see if she had arrived safely? Not if he thought the phones weren't secure. She didn't know how Chris had arranged this, but William somehow had found out about his plans for her with the convent. She would just have to hope that all else hadn't failed.

During this thought process, it was necessary many times to tamp down the urge for self-preservation and jump up and run off, screaming in this case, into the night or deeper into the field. *This* was self-preservation at the primal level, she told herself. Freeze, like the fawn she'd come upon once on a late spring walk. Become part of the landscape. If she moved at all, she risked William hearing. He stood or sat only a few rows away, waiting for her to make the mistake of breaking cover to get away from him.

And where would she go if she got out? The farm truck blocking the road was disabled. Were the men in it dead from the shots she heard? If they weren't, they probably didn't have guns to fend off the pseudo-nuns. She decided the best plan would be to remain where she was and pray Chris and James came looking for the van — and her.

During a noisy gust of wind, she risked sliding a few feet ahead, out of the puddle, fearing her teeth would begin to chatter if she didn't. Pulling her dress down over her bent legs and arranging the concealing wrap to best advantage, she huddled in a miserable little ball to conserve body heat and await death or rescue.

She was soaked to the skin, though, and continued to shiver. Her ankle throbbed, hot and big, out of sync with her fast, shallow breathing and pounding heart. Amazingly, she felt herself falling asleep despite the haze of physical discomfort. Reaction was setting in, she decided. She gave herself up to it, fervently hoping she didn't snore.

She hadn't slept very long before the sounds of voices and engines coming from the road roused her. She hadn't run as far into the field as she had thought. She pulled the wrap away from her eyes, and risked turning her head to look up. The sky, what she could see of it, was lighter now. The rain had stopped and the moon mooned her through the long leaves.

She heard men's voices, pleading. Was it the men in the farm truck? She hoped so. They could tell Chris and James, or whoever was out there, where she had gone and that the nuns with guns had followed her. She wondered briefly what those confused and frightened men's feelings must be. Gun-packing nuns must surely be the ultimate Catholic oxymoron.

Then she heard what she'd been longing to hear, Chris's and James's voices in the flurry of Portuguese words. She wanted to weep with relief. Chris had told her to stay down and let them come to her. No way should she break cover, giving away her location to the men who still lurked in the field with her. Yet, she sucked in her breath when she realized they could ambush Chris and James very easily from this heavy vegetation, if they entered the field looking for her.

Her tiny velvet evening bag was a sodden weight on her left arm, its silk cord wrapped around her wrist in a death grip. She tugged it open and reached inside, searching for anything she might use to help herself or Chris and James. She froze just as her fingertips found two small cylindrical shapes.

Someone was stealthily moving her way,

from the direction of the road. Chris? James? Could William have circled around her while she slept?

'Dutch? Where are you?' She judged that the man's panicked whisper came from the next row over.

The driving nun. Her fingers closed over her mirrored lipstick case and Gato's laser mouse pointer toy in her bag. She must have gathered up the toy with the items she'd swept off the bathroom sink before she left Abundancia. Earlier, when she'd played with Gato, she had been uncomfortably reminded that the pointer toy's red dot, sans mouse outline, looked exactly like the laser sight she'd seen locked in on Chris's forehead the night they'd helped Estrela deliver her colt. It felt like a week ago, yet it had only been forty-eight hours ago.

The sounds of the man's approach were louder now. She eased her head and right arm far enough between two stalks so she could see down the next row. When the advancing, shadowy figure was almost upon her, she made up her mind, pointed the laser toy upward, and pushed in the button. The red dot glowed against the heavy white material of the nun's habit.

'Look down, *gringo*,' she whispered in the deepest, roughest, toughest accented voice she could muster, imitating how Chris rolled the 'r' sound.

The surprise and fear generated by her hoarse voice coming from the area of his feet, along with what he thought was a laser sight locked in on the middle of his crotch, had the desired effect on the nun who had been driving.

He dropped the gun he held, missing her head by inches. 'Mother of God, don't shoot!' he pleaded in a heavy cockney accent.

It was definitely her amorous friend from James's flat. She dared not speak again. If he realized it was a woman, let alone one wielding a cat toy, who held him prisoner, he'd attempt to overpower her. One kick would probably do it.

The red dot jerked when they heard the sounds of someone crashing through the plants close by, away from them, deeper into the field. William was getting away. He'd been hiding so close to her, almost breathing the same air. She wondered if he guessed the voice was hers. If so, why hadn't he come to his cohort's aid? Maybe Dutch had a sense of humor after all. She could vouch for William's dry and ready wit.

She risked two more words, pouring on the macho gruff. 'Turn, *gringo!*'

When the man did a smart about-face, she

crawled into his row and stood up behind him, barely managing to swallow the cry of pain that rose in her throat. Her sprained ankle and the lacerated soles of her feet both weighed heavily in the pain department. She'd lost track of where the gun had fallen and decided to leave it.

She lifted the mirrored lipstick case above her head in her left hand, above the highest level of leaves, she hoped. Her plan was to move toward the road while she rolled the case between her fingers. With luck it would catch and reflect the glow of headlights coming from around the farm truck.

She poked the ex-nun in the back with Gato's toy and they moved forward. She gritted her teeth when her swollen ankle took the weight of her first step and when mud squished into the many cuts where the dried cornstalk stubble had sliced into the soles of her feet.

The voices from the road abruptly stopped. Absolute silence surrounded them, except for tiny swishing sounds that came from everywhere and nowhere and soon encircled them. She debated whether she should identify herself at that point, but if she spoke too soon . . . She kept moving and hoped Chris's men didn't shoot first and ask questions later.

Like spokes on a wheel with the nun as its hub, many extended arms and hands, holding and steadying guns, suddenly poked through the plants around them. She caught only a glimpse because someone tackled her from the left with such force that they crashed through several rows of plants. She and her assailant landed in a heap, with her on the bottom and her face pushed into the wet *cerrados* soil.

Moving lights abruptly bathed the area around them, making leaf shadows dance wildly in the tiny area she could see by peeking under her left armpit. The man on top of her didn't speak, didn't move, yet she felt his alertness. His left wrist, beside her head, wore a gold watch. Chris.

The captured pseudo-nun was venting his feelings, in English, to anyone within earshot. He was especially aggrieved that a fellow soldier would play so unfair as to put the family jewels in harm's way. He wanted to know which one of them it had been. His voice grew fainter, which probably meant some of Chris's men had removed him.

She finally heard Sami's voice say the strange phrase he'd used before at the stable. Chris's quiet answering word rumbled through her back before his weight lifted off her.

Then James was there, kneeling beside her in the dirt. 'Emily? Are you hurt?'

She rose onto her elbows and looked around. She was surrounded by boots. Large boots.

Sami echoed James's concern. 'Tell me where you're hurt, Emily Noble.'

'My right ankle. The bottoms of my feet. My beautiful dress. My dignity. That's all,' she mumbled.

Sami briefly examined her and gave her two tiny, white pills for pain, with a sip of water.

After that, callused hands of all sizes and shapes, lifted her like she was precious, extremely breakable, and weighed nothing at all.

'I'll carry her,' a rough voice said. The hands fell away after transferring her gently to Chris's waiting arms.

'Where's your weapon, Emily?' James asked her.

She ignored him. Shivering, she wrapped her arms like straps around Chris's neck, buried her face against his skin, and hung on, vaguely aware that she still clutched her mirrored lipstick case in one hand and Gato's toy, her weapon, in the other.

'I was s-so scared,' she said, moving her lips against his neck. 'I didn't know if you would

245

come, if you would even know . . . '

His arms tightened around her. 'I pretended to leave then I followed the van. Something didn't feel right.'

Her teeth began to chatter in earnest. 'M-me, too. I n-noticed cigarettes and a lighter in the van. Then I s-saw his ring. I didn't know what to do except to run into a field when they stopped. I did what you taught me to do. I hit the dirt and covered up with my wrap until the cavalry arrived. Then, when you got here and they were getting away, I used Gato's pointer toy like a laser sight to stop the little one, and my mirrored lipstick c-case to show you where we were.'

Chris stopped so abruptly that he skidded in the mud. All the men around them stopped, in fact. She looked around the circle of amazed faces peering at her through the leaves. When her words were translated for those who didn't speak English, looks of fascinated disbelief mixed with horror showed on the rest of their faces. Several men crossed themselves, murmuring.

James was the first to understand and say around a laugh, 'So that's what he was on about. Aimed for the family jewels again, did you?'

Chris looked down at her, his face working. 'You didn't have a gun?'

'No, it's back there in the field somewhere. He almost dropped it on my head.'

She was dumbfounded when Chris threw back his head and roared with laughter.

His men joined in.

'They were all I had with me, so I used them,' she informed him peevishly.

He reined in his emotions and started forward again. 'You made excellent use of your resources. James and I would have been hard-pressed to do as well. And I doubt that we would have thought of using Gato's toy to fake out the cockney or of using a mirrored lipstick case to attract attention to our position.'

'Well, neither of you would've carried either one of those things away with you in an evening bag, accidentally or on purpose, I hope.'

'You are amazing, Emily,' he said, looking down at her.

Her eyes closed because they wouldn't stay open any longer. 'No, I'm not. I'm quite ordinary really. I just react to life in strange ways.'

His words and Sami's pills made her feel light. Before she floated out of his arms, she had to tell him something. Very important.

'William, the grumpy nun, ran away from the road. Eleven o'clock. Five yards from where I went down. I think,' she murmured.

She felt his lips press against her forehead. 'Hush. You're safe now. We'll talk later.' With that, she relaxed and let something deeper than sleep briefly take her.

They drove somewhere. She and Sami and a dark-haired woman she didn't know had a relentless session of packing her ankle in ice and of cleaning her cuts and bandaging her feet. The way events in Brazil were progressing, she was thankful her doctor had insisted on a tetanus booster during her last physical, before she renewed her passport. Sami gave her two more white pills before they took to the road again. She woke up in her bed at Abundancia, with the unknown woman sitting nearby.

Gato was in his usual place at the foot. He made his way up her side to petting range, fretting out loud that she had been gone so long.

She gathered him to her and stared at the woman a moment, fearful. What if last night had been a dream? What if William really . . . 'Who are you?' she croaked.

The woman patted her arm in a reassuring gesture. 'I'm Jovanna DelGado. Those men chased you into one of our fields last night. Chris brought you to our farmhouse because I'm a nurse. I helped Sami clean your cuts and tend to your ankle before they brought you here. I insisted on coming along. And you couldn't keep Giovanni, my husband, away.' She helped Emily sit up, with lots of pillows behind her back.

'Thank you. Where is everyone?'

'They're all in the *sala*, doing what men do after a crisis, drink and compare notes. My husband plays with making wines. A hobby. He gathered up bottles of his most promising vintages for Chris to try. It's dawn and they're still at it.'

James came in, looking tired and a little glassy-eyed.

Jovanna, with a smile, gave her a 'see what I mean' look. 'Well, I'll go pour Giovanni into our vehicle, and we'll head home, now that I'm sure you're all right.' She glanced at James. 'Chris insisted that some of our men follow us in a truck. Tell Chris to bring you for a visit, under more pleasant circumstances.'

She thanked Jovanna for her help and her presence. After she left, Emily held out a hand to James, who took it and kissed the back.

'Are you okay, James?'

'Hey, that's my line.'

'Try this one then. Are the nuns, the real ones, okay?'

'They're fine. Apparently Dutch broke in and took the spare habits from two of their cells while they were at prayers. That older model van would have been easy to hot-wire, but he didn't have to do that. The ignition switch is worn out. It starts without a key. The sisters didn't even know he'd been there until they couldn't find the van to pick you up. Chris says the Reverend Mother is more shocked than upset that a man breached the portals.' His grin cheered her but only briefly.

She asked the burning question: 'How did William know our plans?'

James sighed heavily. 'The cockney has connections in Brazil. He has someone in the wireless phone company who monitored and reported Chris's cell phone calls to the convent. He's bragged that he's rather good at that sort of thing. Dutch cut the lines at the convent. The sisters went to a bar to use the telephone. Chris is buying them a nicer van, for their trouble and for their speed in contacting him.'

She studied her scratched hands then picked at the sheet. 'How's Chris taking all this, now that he's had time to digest it?'

'He's, um, unhappy. Prickly as a hedgehog, in fact. He's been tearing a strip off everyone in sight. I've never seen him like this. He's the coolest man I've ever known in a crisis, but this time . . . ' He looked pointedly at her and grinned.

She squirmed against the pillows. 'Rein in your imagination, brother, and I'll rein in mine. Since Maria of Rio, Chris doesn't commit to, or trust, any woman, and you know how important that is to me. I'm not looking for an affair.' A change in subject was definitely called for. 'Chris said he followed the van.'

'He was on the radio, telling me to get my ass next to his, when the Reverend Mother called his cell phone number to tell him the van and two habits were missing. He ordered all of us back then.'

James sat down on the edge of the bed, taking her hand again, examining the damage this time. 'Chris actually took hold of me and slammed me against the Land Rover door when I got out at the rendezvous point, around the curve from the farm truck. He'd asked me to check out everything at Paulo's and I let him down. He feels that all of us let you down.'

'Don't believe it, James. You three were trying to take me out of danger. And they made pretty good nuns, in the dark and in a van.'

'They did, didn't they? Very non-chatty nuns. I can't believe I tried to have a

251

conversation with Dutch while he was wearing nun drag and sitting in a stolen convent van. He could have dropped me right there. He could have dropped all of us.'

'I wonder why he didn't?'

'Chris thinks it was because you were there and too many of our men were around us. Not only does Dutch want you, but he wants you out of harm's way.' He swallowed. 'Chris believes strongly now that Dutch hopes you don't know about his past life, and that we haven't made the connection with his current one. If he stashes you somewhere out of danger then rescues you as William Vanders, you might look favorably upon him. Especially if we're dead and out of his way.'

She shuddered, at both thoughts. 'Did you get anything out of the driving nun about William's plans?'

'Not a lot. Chris, Giovanni, and I questioned him while Sami and Jovanna worked on you last night. And Chris has updated his friend Marcos, the police commander he talked to when Miguel was killed at the silos. Apparently, Marcos is intelligent, sensible, a former school chum, and an old family friend. He realizes that Abundancia is too far from Barreiras for the police to be effective, although your attempted kidnapping happened in his backyard.

'Chris has been the law around Abundancia for many years, a deputy or a constable or the Brazilian equivalent of the same, so Marcos is letting Chris call the shots on this situation. He's taking it on faith and Chris's word that Dutch is a murderer.'

'Show him the pictures.' She squeezed James's hand. 'I want to hear everything that happened after you and Chris and the men found the van. I heard voices but I couldn't understand them or figure out what was going on.'

'Well, by the time we made our cautious way around the curve to the van, you had long vanished into the field and Dutch and his friend had followed you.'

'Are the men in the farm truck all right? I heard William or the other one shoot at them.'

'They're fine, physically, but I doubt they'll ever be the same again. First, nuns fire on them. Then Chris appears, wild-eyed and out for blood. They begged him for mercy. I've never seen him like that. We made Chris stand away from them so we could calm them down. He was furious, but we couldn't get any sense out of them otherwise.

'Chris was setting up a sweep of the field with our men when we saw your mirror flashing.' He smiled, looking like he was ten years old again. 'Nice use of the resources you had on your person, Em.'

'Don't call her Em.' Chris's voice coming from the doorway startled both of them.

James, acting guilty as sin, leaped off his perch on the edge of the bed. When he realized what he'd done, he grinned at her, looking sheepish. Emily made a mental note to pry into just how many times he'd been caught in or on a bed he had no right to be in or on.

'Don't you start as well,' he said to Chris, betrayal in every word.

Chris's eyes were fixed on her. 'She doesn't like it and neither do I.'

'I see. Well then,' James conceded.

'Go tell Sami he wants you,' Chris suggested.

'No need to be subtle. If you want another word with Emily, just say so. Only no shouting this time, please. I'm feeling rather fragile after sampling Giovanni's — '

Chris tore his gaze away from her and pointed it at James, who quickly left the room. Not wanting to be alone with Chris, she raised a hand to stop her brother, words of protest hovering on her lips. Instead, she said nothing and let her hand drop limply onto the sheet.

# 15

The silence between them was deafening. She was desperate to break it, preferably on a light note. 'Last night went well, don't you think?'

He returned her grin. 'Didn't it, though? If things get any worse, I'll have to ask you to stop helping me.'

She continued with a little chuckle. 'Did the driving nun tell you anything you can use?'

'The driving nun's name is Harry, or rather, 'Arry. He didn't know anything, but he talked a lot. He's a merc from a private military company in England. That's what they call them these days. He's a computer expert so Dutch must have brought him in to hack into James's computer. And having a girlfriend in Brasilia, his friend at the telephone company, probably put his stock up with Dutch. Harry didn't know Dutch before he recruited him for this private job. Dutch told him it was personal business. And I can tell you he's not the caliber of soldier Dutch usually associates with.'

Anger and disgust colored her words. 'Well, I think Harry is a thoroughly nasty, oversexed little man who doesn't recognize the difference between a hit man and a soldier. By the way, he's the same man who was in James's flat. I recognized his voice.'

She watched Chris's fists clench at his sides. 'He admitted that. He said Dutch was blown away when you turned up there and that he disguised his voice after that. It was a long shot, luring you to England to get to James, but one Dutch was willing to take. I think we made it clear to our cockney friend that Dutch would have killed him, too, when he was no longer useful. We left him under heavy guard in one of Giovanni's outbuildings. Marcos is sending someone to pick him up.'

A shiver crawled over her, but she squared her shoulders. 'James says you're tearing a strip off everyone in sight. If it's my turn, may we get on with it, please, because I can't stand the suspense. And I'd like it to go on the record that I'm tired of having these little discussions of ours while I'm in bed.'

His swift response brought heat to her cheeks. 'And I'm tired of fighting this desire to join you in your bed because I'm failing miserably at it.'

He approached, and his voice changed to exasperated and stern. 'And since you brought it up, it's most definitely your turn.

That was a damned foolish thing you did, Emily. Brave, but foolish. You took on a trained, and warped, soldier with a cat toy and a mirrored lipstick case. What possessed you?'

'He would have gotten away if I hadn't stopped him somehow. I thought that removing Harry might be useful to you in a couple of ways. We've deprived William of his services, and I hoped Harry might tell you something you didn't already know. He was the only thing I could salvage out of that situation that might help end this . . . siege on our lives. I knew by his voice that the man coming toward me wasn't William. Trust me, I wouldn't have had the courage to do it if it had been William coming down that row.'

'I'm glad to hear it.'

When silence descended again, she ventured, 'I know I ask this a lot, but what happens now?'

With the toe of one of his boots, he followed the fringed edge of the throw rug on the floor beside the bed. 'We've been discussing that. I wasn't thinking clearly last night. I just wanted to bring you home where I could protect you. Now that we're here, I realize I can't. Nothing has changed.

'So, you're still leaving us. Like James, I don't want my past life to touch you any more than it already has. You can't stay here or at the convent. We place in danger anyone we ask to help us, so we couldn't leave you with Giovanni and Jovanna, although they insisted on coming back here with us. Harry might be a target risk now, so I don't want you anywhere near him.'

He took her passport out of his khaki pants pocket and handed it to her. 'Pack the rest of your clothes. We'll hide you in your rental car. James, disguised as a worker, will drive it to Barreiras, deliver you to the police, then hand in your car to the rental agency. One pickup truck with a cap on the bed and some men inside will follow the car to bring him back.'

'You're sending me away like an unwelcome parcel.'

He continued as though she hadn't spoken. 'Marcos will put you on a plane to the States. I'm sending you to my mother in Georgia until this is over, one way or the other.'

She continued her thought until what he'd said sank in. 'An unwelcome parcel that you're handing off to . . . your mother? I'd love to meet her, but won't I put her in danger?'

'It's another calculated risk. The danger is here because Dutch is here. The time allotted for his little hunting trip is almost over. He'll have to end this soon. Maybe he'll get careless.'

'Or maybe you will.' She gulped.

'I promise you I won't.' He sat down in James's place on the bed and reached across her legs to pet Gato, stretched out full-length beside her. 'Do you remember the proposition you put to me in the courtyard?'

'The children's books about Abundancia?' If he was this close to her then she had to touch him, she couldn't help herself. She reached out and took his right hand, comparing her left one's size and finger length when she put them palm against palm.

'When it's safe, will you come back to Abundancia to work on the books?' He locked his fingers with hers.

'Is that all I'll be coming back for?' she asked, a little catch in her voice.

He leaned closer. 'We'll have to explore the possibilities. Together. I don't pretend to understand or to want what's happening between us, but I've figured out a few details. I know you make me feel emotions I swore I'd never allow myself to feel again. I know that at Paulo's last night, your heart spoke to mine. I know I intend to claim what your heart offered me then.'

She remembered the moment of stillness between them, remembered what had been in

259

her heart. Did he really know? 'And what did *you* hear my heart offer, Christovao Santos?'

He closed the gap between them. Each word, accompanied by a feather light kiss, sounded like a prayer in the quiet room. 'Sanctuary. Refuge. Peace.'

Her amazement at his repeating the words she'd said to him without speaking was lost in a new wonder, his long, deep kiss, which quickened every pore. So sensitive was she to his touch this morning that she felt the tiny ridges of his fingertips on her face as she tasted his lips on hers.

'Will you come back? Will you try to work here?' he murmured against her mouth before he pulled back. 'But you'll have to bring James as a chaperone, because I won't be able to keep my hands off you otherwise. I've been afflicted this way since the moment you shot at me.'

'My shooting at you is not a favorite memory.' She smiled inside, not letting it show. 'I plead fever. What if I'd hit what I was really aiming at?'

His facial expression was priceless.

'Just kidding. And I somehow can't imagine James as a chaperone.'

'I owe you for that one.' He gave an exaggerated sigh of relief. 'James as chaperone does stretch the imagination a bit. Leave him in England then and take your chances.'

So, it would be her choice but his terms. That was plain enough. The gut-wrenching, brain-numbing attraction between them was there, no doubt about it, but she doubted she'd ever hear Christovao Santos tell her in this lifetime that he felt anything for her other than desire.

She shrugged. 'I'll think about it. I'll be ready to leave as soon as I'm dressed,' she said tonelessly and leaned back against the pillows.

He took a long look at the white eyelet nightgown, which she wore thanks to Jovanna's help. 'I like what you're wearing now.'

She pulled the sheet higher and again attempted to turn the conversation before it took them places she wouldn't risk going. 'Brazil is certainly hard on a girl's clothes. I'm sorry about the dress. Jovanna and I decided there's no chance of saving it.'

Her words had the desired, distracting, irritating effect. He stood up and headed for the door. 'Maybe Maria of Rio will make another one like it for you sometime. I'll ask her.'

After he left, she dressed in jeans and a regular-length T-shirt, easing her feet into her running shoes. She loosely tied them so she wouldn't trip over the laces. The dressed cuts on her feet and her swollen ankle, which was wrapped in an elastic bandage, weren't as painful this morning as she had feared they might be. She became aware of the sounds of voices and of engines running in the compound behind the house. By the time she was ready, Gato's fur was wet with her tears.

Manoel waited outside her door. He took the second bag Chris had loaned her and escorted her through the *sala* to the compound. She hugged him good-bye.

James reappeared as a dirty, scowling farmworker beneath a floppy hat. He ushered her to her rental car and stuffed her into the backseat, covering her with clean grain sacks.

The compound was strangely quiet, she noticed, with no roof guards visible when she peeped out from under her sacks. Chris and Sami weren't around either when they drove through the gates, which James left open behind them. She heard no second vehicle following them. She was thankful James was with her, yet her fear that she might never see Chris again almost choked her.

They were on the road half an hour when slight nausea made her speak from the tiny backseat where she was curled. 'James, I have to sit upright, or I'll be sick.'

'Did you bring your hat?'

She had both the hat and the sunglasses in her bag. She put them on and clambered between the bucket seats to the front. She glanced behind them. 'Will Manoel follow to bring you back?'

He scowled at the road ahead, at last sitting up tall. He had been slouching behind the wheel to make himself appear shorter, just as William had done in the van. 'No, he won't. Change of plans. Chris sent Turk's manuscript, papers, and pictures with me today to hand over to the police. Once you're on the plane, Chris's friend Marcos will release the contents to the worldwide media. Dutch's cover in your world will be blown. He can never go back to his William Vanders persona, or to you, as William. Chris wants me to come back here with Marcos.'

She reeled with the magnitude of what Chris was doing. 'And what's the plan at Abundancia now?' He didn't speak, so she repeated her question.

Anger colored his words when he answered. 'The plan is very like what you once described. He sent the guards, Mei, everyone, away and told me to leave the gates open. Didn't you notice? He's inviting Dutch in for a showdown. He believes it will be over, one way or another, by the time I get back with Marcos.'

'Oh, God,' she moaned. Now she realized why Chris had sent James with her instead of sending one of his men. It was because of her plea last night for her brother's safety. Chris's noble gesture just might get him killed, and it would be her fault.

She caught her breath on a sob. 'Go back, James. Help them. You fought together at Cheneyville. You should stand together here.'

'My thoughts exactly.' The car slowed. 'Will you promise me you'll go on to Barreiras with the manuscript, to the police? Promise me!'

She gulped. 'It will probably shorten my life by years, but I promise.'

He executed a U-turn on the narrow farm road and floored the gas pedal. The return journey, fraught with tension, felt twice as long. When they neared the field closest to the house, he stopped the car.

'I'll go on foot from here. Turn this car around, Emily, and don't look back. No matter what.' He pulled his gun from his leg holster, kissed her, and jumped out. Hugging the edge of the field, he loped off in the direction of the house.

Sobbing now, she did what her brother had ordered her to do, dashing tears from her eyes as she performed her own U-turn and pointed the car north.

Silent tears continued to roll down her

cheeks ten minutes later when she sat up straight and jerked around to look to her right. Something had glinted in the sunlight in the field beside her, something that shouldn't be there.

She stopped the car and reversed slowly. When she saw the flash again, she stalled the engine in her eagerness to jump out and high-step into the chest-high plants. With trembling hands she pulled them aside to see what someone had hidden there.

A dusty, brand-new, powerful monster of a motorcycle, its metal ticking in the warm, clear sunshine, was imperfectly camouflaged by the lush growth. A flattened trail of plants angled up to it, showing that its owner had ridden it into the field from another direction. The machine was spotted with dew or rain, but one shining spot of chrome gleamed where someone had accidentally rubbed it clean while walking around it.

William Vanders collected motorcycles, the bigger and more powerful the better. The sight of his ostentatious possession, blood-red and expensive, in Chris's green, humble field made her view it through a crimson haze of rage. The loss of life, the waste, the fear, the pain of William's vendetta rapidly came together in this object. She shoved it over onto its side, gave the machine a good kick with her left foot, took its key, and flung it as hard and as far as she was able. If William Vanders was the only one left standing at the end of this day then the bastard could walk home.

As she glared at the huge machine, which reminded her of a giant, colorful, overturned beetle that couldn't right itself, she heard the pieces of her broken promise to James settle around her as lightly as ash from a cigarillo. She had to go back. She couldn't bear not knowing what was happening to them.

She kicked the machine once more, on general principles, before she turned away. That physical release allowed her to examine another reason for going back. If Chris and James were going to die today, then she wanted to be with them. How could she summon up any enthusiasm for life if they weren't here to share it with her? How could she look forward to the future if Chris and his violet-eyed babies weren't part of it? On any terms he chose. If none of it was meant to be, then let it end here, with all of them together.

She hid Turk's manuscript, now in a plastic document case, in the field across the road. She built a little pyramid of stones at the edge of the road and gouged a mark in the dirt with the heel of her shoe to mark the row, then turned the car south for the second time that day, toward Abundancia.

She'd have to get the car as close to the house as possible because of her ankle. She accelerated before she left the cover of the last field then switched off the engine and let the vehicle coast, steering around the outer wall to the back of the compound. She inched the rental close to the wall and climbed out the passenger side. She left the door hanging open, not wanting to risk the sound of its closing.

The little car's metal shell was hot beneath her shoe soles as she climbed onto the trunk then up onto the roof, no mean feat. From that vantage point, she peeked over the top of the wall near the stable. The compound was as silent and as unmoving as a still life. The horses had probably been turned out on this extraordinarily fine day, perhaps even left out to enjoy last night's heavy rain. At least they weren't stomping around inside the building, complaining.

She hauled herself over the wall and dropped to the ground on the other side, stifling a cry of pain when her feet and ankle protested her cavalier treatment. From the cover of the empty stable, she studied the compound and what was visible at the back of the house. Nothing stirred. She heard no sounds except the drone of farm machines in the distance. Life went on elsewhere, unaware of the danger unfolding at Abundancia.

She didn't have a plan, and she was aware that she was unarmed, though not defenseless. James had told her once that she would never be defenseless as long as she could speak or scream. But even her pockets were empty this go-round.

The men in and around Abundancia under siege had always appeared to drip weapons and firepower, but she didn't know where the arsenal was kept. The only weapons in plain sight, the spears on the wall in the *sala*, would be useless to her. She'd probably impale herself, but she didn't have any other choice.

The *sala* would be her goal for that reason and because that's where she might find Chris and James and Sami. She didn't know exactly which room was the bull's-eye for today's operation. Offhand, she couldn't think of anything clever she might say when she presented herself to them. But it would have to be good. And short. Because it would be difficult to speak at all with Chris's fingers around her throat.

The outer compound offered her no cover. She ran low, in a limping scuttle, across the open space in record time. The chest-high wall of the inner courtyard and the young trees surrounding the terrace now shielded her from the house and from the four sets of double doors across the back, two into the *sala* and one each into the library and Chris's study. She moved to the corner, edged a hip up onto a nearby planter, pulled herself up, and swung over, thereby avoiding the gate's squeak.

The first set of screened double doors into the *sala* stood open to the terrace. Her shoes made no sound on the flag-stones as she made her way to a sweet-smelling, flowering shrub growing in one of the huge pots near the doors. As she approached its cover, a familiar voice came from behind her.

'Good morning, Emily.' Instead of making her jump, the clipped, carefully enunciated words froze her in mid-step. William. Dutch. Willem. Little fingers of fear began stroking her mind. She forced herself to think calmly. If he didn't kill her on the spot, maybe she could stall until the others figured out what she'd foolishly done. Maybe she could create a diversion, or warn them, or simply occupy William to give them an edge, an opportunity. Maybe she could gain a little time by pretending she thought William was paying her a surprise visit. Or maybe this was her last minute on earth.

She slowly turned on legs that wobbled and pasted a sickly, surprised smile on her face.

One glance and her smile slipped off, her mouth dropped open, and she abandoned the doomed deception.

She wouldn't have known this action-figure wannabe as William Vanders, dressed as he was for the part. His hair was cut military short so that it stood straight up in a silvery white aura around his head. His tall, lean, muscular body was clothed from head to toe in camouflage twills, including a sweatband around his forehead. In his left hand, close to his left thigh, he held a gun with a long, slim extension on the muzzle. Even she recognized a silencer when she saw one. From a scabbard that was threaded onto his web belt, the handle of a huge knife protruded.

On a jarring note, he wore glasses with pinkish-orange lenses. Shooting lenses, James had called them. He looked her up and down through them while she did the same with him. She was thankful she didn't have to look into those cruel, pale eyes again.

'Not your usual buttoned-down look, William,' she rasped, her throat suddenly dry. 'War games?'

He smiled at her. He actually had a slow, very pleasant smile, for a snake. 'In a manner of speaking. You should have acted surprised, Emily. You should have pretended. I'll miss your wit, you know. You always say the most unexpected things to me. I regret that you became entangled in this.'

He grasped her elbow, spun her around, and marched her ahead of him into the *sala*. She went limp with relief when she saw that the huge room was empty.

He scanned the space, his gun at the ready, while guiding her away from the doors. 'It's my fault, really. My hired help failed when James turned out to be so elusive. It was my decision to take over his kill and use you to flush him out. If you had cooperated in London, we could have avoided this. After James conveniently made his way to Brazil and you followed, I tried to remove you to safety a second time.'

'As a heavily armed nun wearing combat boots? The habit didn't do you justice, William.'

'Thank you. Please remember that I tried to save you, Emily, really I did, but you are a contrary woman. I knew you were in that car somewhere today, and I was willing to let you go. You should have continued on to Barreiras. What made you come back?'

'Your motorcycle glinted, flaunting itself, in one of Chris's fields. I recognized your taste in machines and decided my place was with my brother for the little going away party you've planned for him and the others.'

His restless gaze continued to search the room. 'Touché. So you know the whole story. Too bad. I didn't recognize James at first. I really thought he was one of Santos's peons. I should mention that James won't be joining us.'

She felt her blood drain from her extremities as her fingers contracted into claws. An animal sound filled her throat as she turned and launched herself at his face. Before she laid one fingernail on him, she found herself facing the other way, with his right arm beneath her breasts and his gun against her left temple.

'I knew it,' he said huskily into her ear. 'When I saw you out there on the terrace, I hoped you'd be like this, fighting me every step of the way. I knew you wouldn't go quietly into death. And do you know what, Emily? Knowing that turns me on. Just like your turning me down always did.'

Tears spilled down her cheeks. 'Turns you on? You bastard, I'd like to turn you inside out! Do you remember what I said to you in London? Well you can — '

He squeezed the breath out of her while he laughed and cupped her left breast. 'Calm down and be nice to me, Emily. James is having a little rest in one of the outbuildings until he's needed. Now, where do you think our friend Hawk might be?'

Not dead. Oh, thank God. James wasn't dead. Yet.

They were facing the bar. The symmetry of the staggered, yet even, display on the wall behind it was out of kilter. It took her another second to figure out that one of them was missing, the horrific spear that belonged to Sami. And to his father before him, she added, because one thing was never said, or thought; without the other.

She felt a spurt of hope. Sami had a personal score to settle with William. If he had taken down the spear that meant so much to him, then he intended to use it. And she didn't doubt that Chris was deadly in his own right.

'I'm waiting, Emily,' William breathed into her ear. 'God, how I've missed you. I haven't had a good conversation since I left you in New York.'

Where would Chris and Sami make their stand? Where would Chris want William to go, other than straight to hell, hold the handbasket? Of course. Where he and Sami had led her that fateful night she'd come to Abundancia. To the only room that, by design, had shown a light.

# 16

'Chris's study,' she whispered.

'One thing, Emily, before we go there and things become . . . unpleasant for you.'

He swung her around to face him, holding her close to him, his right arm around her waist. His body was hard and cold against hers. She could have gotten the same sensation by hugging a boulder.

After a few seconds of studying her face and hair, as if memorizing them, he continued. 'An admission given because you won't live to use the power you hold over me. I never loved anyone or anything until I met you. I didn't think myself capable of it.'

Shock slammed into her and she sucked in her breath, her lips parting slightly. His eyes were on them.

'I don't like the feeling, and it makes you a danger to me. At times you've made me wish to the bottom of my black soul that I was a different man than I am. You've even made me wonder if my life would have been different if I'd met you sooner. I can't afford to think like that, and it presents me with an interesting little dilemma. I wonder if I can kill you when the time comes.' His eyes were hard now behind the tinted lenses.

She spoke the words as they came to her — and packed them in ice. 'Oh, I'm sure you'll manage, William. Just be true to your personal code. No survivors.'

'Have a care, my love.' An edge crept into his voice, like that on a newly honed knife. 'You've only glimpsed the other side of my personality. Remember me in London. Remember me in the cornfield. Treat me well.'

He smiled at her involuntary gasp. In response, he lifted the gun to her temple and started a slow descent down her jawline to the right side of her neck, where blood pulsed. She stared into his eyes and defied him. He might be the last thing she ever saw in this life, but he couldn't control her thoughts, where Chris and James and her parents lived.

'That's my girl,' he whispered then kissed her where the cool metal had begun its descent, her temple. His lips were even colder than she remembered. She was glad when he spun her around again to face away from him.

He kept his back against the house, with her as a shield in front of him, as they moved along the terrace then trampled through flower beds, making their way to the study. When they came to the second set of double doors into the sala, and then the set into the library, he swung around each time so she faced the openings.

The study was empty when they stepped inside. She couldn't believe her eyes. Turk's black leather portfolio lay on Chris's cleared desktop, like X marked the spot. Or the bull's-eye.

'We'll wait. I'm sure he'll be along soon. Please don't do anything stupid, Emily.'

He'd dragged a chair from in front of Chris's desk to the center of the room and pushed her into it. Then he prowled the space, closing the terrace doors and pulling the draperies across, while Emily, feeling like a fly caught in a spider's web, watched and waited.

He toed the splintered section of hardwood floor. 'Santos is getting old. Accidental discharge of a weapon?'

'No, I did it. I shot at him to get his attention when he wouldn't take me seriously.'

He stared at her a moment before he shook his head and smiled. 'You're one of a kind, Emily. And how did you get Harry to surrender? That was you, disguising your voice, in the field?'

'Yes, it was me. Why didn't you help him if you knew that?'

'I decided to let you have him. A little gift. Harry had outlived his usefulness to me, and he didn't know anything that would help Santos. Answer me. How did you get him to surrender?'

When she told him about the laser cat toy and the mirrored lipstick case, he repeated, 'One of a kind. Fortunately for me.' After that, she was aware of him periodically glancing at the floor, then at her with a smile.

She spent the time berating herself. Instead of being in a position to help Chris and Sami, or to just stay quietly out of their way, she was now a giant handicap to them, in William's power like this. What could she do sitting in a chair in the middle of the room, except present an easy target? If, by some miracle they survived this, Chris would probably enjoy putting her on a plane himself because of her stupidity and her overconfidence.

She became conscious of a commonplace sound, growing louder in the unnatural quiet that hung over Abundancia, a sound that made her rigid with fear. Firm footsteps, at a steady pace on the tile walk, approached the study.

'Shhh,' William advised, and the look that

accompanied it made her bite back her warning shout.

She held her breath, the tension building until she thought she would scream. Each second was a minute long. Every sound, every movement was magnified, amplified a hundred times: the footsteps she could not mistake, the angry buzz of a bee ricocheting around the ceiling, the slow, cold smile that grew on William's face before he slipped behind her chair.

The footsteps stopped outside the study door. 'I'm coming in, Dutch. Unarmed.'

'I don't believe you, but come,' William responded.

When Chris entered the room, William's left hand rested on her shoulder with the gun's length resting on her left breast. Chris flinched then paled as his eyes briefly locked with hers. She saw despair, fear, anger . . . and something else in them. Something hungry. He was in warrior mode, and the cold calculation she'd seen once before was there briefly. His glance shot from her to the face she was sure still smiled above her. Where was Sami? Turk's portfolio on the desk indicated they had a plan. Was it salvageable now that she had blundered into it?

William's voice was as slow and as cold as his smile had been. 'If you have any weapons,

Hawk, get rid of them. Now. For her sake. Do you take my meaning?'

Chris gave a nod of understanding. She didn't want to know the details of the unspoken pact they'd just made. She assumed it had something to do with the quickness of her death.

'I have no weapons,' he said.

'Good. So, Hawk, what do you think of my Emily?' William extended his thumb away from the gun's grip and slowly drew it up then down her cheek. 'As if I don't already know.'

Chris's calmness fled. He snarled an ugly Portuguese word and took a step forward.

In a blink the weapon pointed at Chris. 'Not yet, Hawk,' William said softly.

She watched the gun right above her left shoulder, first in her peripheral vision, then out of the corner of her eye. If she just brought her arm up . . .

'Emily,' Chris warned, still breathing heavily. He held her eyes with the intensity of someone trying to force understanding.

She heard amusement in William's voice. 'You are incorrigible, Emily, but I suggest you listen to him.' To Chris, he said, 'Where's that servant of yours?'

Emily shot a look of wide-eyed disbelief at Chris. Servant? She realized he meant Sami, but calling Sami a servant was like calling an assault rifle a water pistol. If that was how William thought of Sami, then he'd made a deadly mistake.

'I sent the servants away. If you were watching, you saw the mass exodus a while ago. No one is here but us. Isn't that the way you wanted it?'

'Until James arrived. Then Emily. I'll catch up with him later.' William motioned with the gun that Chris should come forward to stand beside Emily's chair. He edged away on the other side, positioning himself near the desk. Exactly where she had stood the night Sami . . .

'You didn't answer me, Hawk, but I know.' He then trained his gun and his comments on her. 'I was on the silos that night, waiting with my night scope, because I know Hawk's an early riser. Then I caught an unexpected late show. I saw him kiss you. And you kissed him back, didn't you?

'Your presence, especially so near my target, distracted me, Emily, as it always does. Your performance made me angry. I should have waited. It took me a long time to line up that shot, and you ruined it. You actually saved him. What am I going to do with you?'

Chris's look had told her that something was in the works. The more time she bought them, the better their chance of survival.

She swallowed her distaste and spoke. 'For one thing, you can satisfy my curiosity about a small point. May I ask you something?'

He relaxed, smiling with surprise and gratification. 'Of course. What would you like to know?'

*That's it*, she coaxed him silently, *let down your guard, just a little*. 'That night you were on the silos you escaped into a tall field, then later, as a nun, you somehow got out of another tall field. You used the fields today for cover for your motorcycle and for yourself. They're vast. How do you do it without getting lost in them?'

He appeared delighted to enlighten her. 'I carry a handheld GPS unit, Global Positioning System. Don't leave home without it in the *cerrados*. Are you trying to distract me, Emily? I'm sorry, my love, but it really is too late. You should have let me save you when you had the chance.'

He pointed the gun at Chris again. 'Now it's my turn to be curious. Did Emily tell you about my interest in her, Hawk?'

She couldn't see Chris's face, but its expression must have been telling.

'I thought so. Like you, I've never had trouble getting any woman I wanted, until Emily here blew into my life and blew my mind with her fantastic illustrations and her great legs. She wouldn't let me get close to her. She wouldn't let me in. But she kisses you like that? What's going on here? I asked myself, and I guessed the correct answer. But I digress.'

Emily closed her eyes, fearing he might see confirmation of her love for Chris in them. When she opened them again, she concentrated on William's camouflage boots. His feet were small for a man of his height, and narrow like a boy's. He'd confided to her that it bothered him. She wondered if he'd bought these killing boots in his usual half-size larger, filling them out with several pairs of socks. When the boots shifted, she looked up. She was thankful that his eyes were on Chris.

'I assume you both know the whole story behind this little hunting trip of mine? Where are Turk's papers? They were the catalyst in all this, you know, along with my finding out Emily's brother is James King.'

She studied this new William and was swept by the sensation that she was seeing a negative image. In this pale, warped man dwelled shadows, pale images, of missing parts that would have made him human. Beside her stood a clear picture of a whole man, complete with regrets and remorse.

'It was quite a shock, Emily, seeing James

with you that day, on the heels of finding out from another publisher that he'd bought a tell-all, an expose, by an ex-mercenary about a massacre in Africa. It wasn't my week. I almost didn't get out of my office in time.'

Chris's voice was low, intense. 'Let her go, Dutch. Turk's dead. His papers never have to see the light of day. You can go back to your old life. She won't have any proof — '

'You mean the old, good life you screwed over because you fought to keep me from taking the second truck at Cheneyville?' William's neutral expression dissolved into a maniacal mask. 'You wouldn't let me steal it and you wouldn't die. You owe me a couple of million dollars, you big Brazilian bastard.'

She watched William, as tense as Gato ready to pounce on an ant, fight to regain control. And he did, like he'd flipped a switch.

'The papers don't matter, really. Cheneyville is a moot point now. I gave up on Turk's book when I saw James leave earlier with Emily tucked away. I assume it's in her car or somewhere along the road, but I doubt I'll bother to look for it. I didn't follow them because I decided to concentrate on you, Hawk. Cut off the head, so to speak. I've been in one of your outbuildings, inside your compound, since before dawn. I beat

283

you home, in fact.

'I've moved on to Plan C. I took the precaution of setting up another life elsewhere before I started this. Third time, charm. The William life wouldn't be any fun anyway without Emily.'

'Let her go,' Chris ordered. 'What's the point? She won't know who or what you are in your new life.'

'I won't let her go, because she loves you instead of me. But I have the satisfaction of knowing she hasn't slept with you, either, and now she never will. I'm aware of Emily's views on love, you see. And yours.'

'William, please,' she heard herself say as heat rose in her cheeks. 'You're going to murder me, but do you have to embarrass me first?'

He smiled gently at her and said, 'Sorry, my love. You're the only woman I know who blushes. I'm glad I saw your last one.'

He returned his attention to Chris. 'I'll make the scenario a neat little double murder and suicide for the star-crossed lovers and the brother. She turned you down, too, and you couldn't take it. Not after the last one. The police can accept it or reject it.' His smile never reached his eyes this time. 'You'll have to watch her die, Hawk.'

Emily felt Chris tense beside her. They had

run out of time. Where the hell was Sami? Her untrained eye measured the open space Chris would have to cross to reach William. If they both went for him . . .

A reflected movement in the sand-filled crystal bowl, bristling with upright cigarillo butts on Chris's desk, drew her eyes. The cavalry?

She quickly brought her attention back to William's face. His gaze was pulling away from her toward the place where she had been looking.

'A bee,' she said, her voice compelling him to concentrate on her. 'I'm afraid of bees. *You* know that. Chris doesn't,' she added softly.

She put it all in her eyes. Everything she might have been to him, the good times they'd shared in the past, the irony of the pie up God's wide sleeve that had brought all of them together in this room. She put the whole emotional buffet, an abundance, on display for him to pick, choose, and share with her.

He blinked then swallowed. 'In a moment, you need fear nothing.' But the gun aimed at her forehead wavered ever so slightly.

Without warning, time and motion stalled, like an unseen hand had pushed the slow-motion button. Frame by inexorable frame, she saw William's face go slack and his knees buckle. She watched in fascination as a gaudy crimson flower with a hard, shiny red stamen bloomed, petal by petal, where the front of his camouflage shirt had been a moment before. Its petals were opening wider when Chris shoved her off her soft chair onto the hard floor. *This is where I came in,* she thought wildly.

In the next heartbeat, William's gun thumped in the silent room. She sensed rather than saw the bullet strike the back of her chair. William fell forward with a sickening thud onto the tropical hardwood floor in front of her. The long, thick, carved shaft of Sami's spear jutted from the middle of his back.

She looked beyond it. An opening had silently appeared in the wall beside and behind Chris's desk. Sami filled the secret doorway, naked to the waist and with a look of utter triumph on his dark face. He raised his arms above his head, lifted his face to the heavens, and opened his throat in a cry of pain and victory that froze Emily's blood. Its echoes rang in her ears, so she covered them and curled into a ball on Mei's shiny floor.

She heard Chris's voice, muffled by her fingers, a second later. 'Cutting it a little fine, weren't you?'

And Sami's low, slow reply. 'It was more difficult than I had thought. But now I can go home. Thank you.'

Someone gently prodded her and she opened her eyes. 'Are we dead?'

'Sami, take his weapons.' Chris's face swam into focus above her. 'We're very much alive and if I didn't have so many things to do, I'd prove it. Are you okay? Come on. Let's get you out of here.'

With a little cry, she threw her arms around his neck. He lifted her in his arms and carried her out of the room, their progress accompanied by her litany of pleas: 'Forgive me, forgive me, forgive me.'

He took her to the *sala*, grabbed the brandy decanter from behind the bar, and sat down with her on the sofa, cradling her like a child, all the while whispering to her softly in Portuguese.

He tipped brandy into her mouth three times then took a long swig from the decanter.

Her trembling wouldn't stop. 'I thought we were going to die. I thought I had killed us all.'

'*He* would have killed us all. It's over now, although Sami's timing was too tight to suit me. He was preparing himself when I left him. There was no safe way to disarm Dutch

287

once you were there, Emily. He left us no choice.'

'I know. I saw how he was. But you offered Sami his chance to revenge his mother and sisters before you came into the study?' At his nod, she asked, 'And you knew I was with William in the study, didn't you? You weren't surprised when you saw me.'

'Before we went to Paulo's, we set up and tested mini remote security cameras inside and outside the house, with viewing monitors in the command center, a small room between the secret doors in the library and the study,' he explained. 'We turned the equipment on when we got back, after Dutch was in place, apparently.'

'I'm sorry I blundered into your plan, but I couldn't stay away, not knowing. I promise I'll be good the rest of my life to make it up to you.' She gave an exhausted shudder and the shaking stopped.

'It would make a change, a boring change.' He patted her bottom. 'I couldn't believe it when I saw you on the monitors. The moment Dutch appeared behind you was one of the worse moments of my life. But he didn't murder you outright, and you took him to the study, where I was supposed to confront him anyway, so we decided to go ahead with a revised plan. Originally, I was the decoy, along with a copy of Turk's manuscript. Sami was the ambush. Neither of us expected you or James to show up.'

She sat bolt upright on his lap. 'James!'

'Sami will bring him here. We had audio, so we heard.'

She struggled to get out of his arms. 'But what if William lied? What if he — ?'

She broke off when James walked into the *sala*. His head was bleeding and he seemed a little woozy, but she flung herself into his arms anyway.

His expression was stern, in an unfocused sort of way. 'You promised me, Emily. Why did you come back?'

'Because I found William's flashy motorcycle, his 'get-away car,' hidden in one of the fields, and it made me so damned angry I couldn't see straight, let alone think properly. I decided that if you two were going to die, then I wanted to be with you. I'm sorry, James.'

Sami, who now wore a shirt, stood uncertainly behind them, his dark eyes on Emily's face, awaiting judgment. She caught a glimpse of his astonished expression when he got the same treatment.

'Thank you, Sami, twice for my life, twice for Chris's life, and twice for James's life. May you live in peace and visit often, or better yet, just stay here with us,' she said softly before letting him go.

'I will visit.' He gave one brief nod, accompanied by a tiny smile, then he turned to Chris. 'I'm taking James to his room to examine him more thoroughly. He has a slight concussion, I think. The men are coming back in small groups, and Marcos is on his way.'

'Thanks, Sami. I'll be along shortly,' Chris said.

'And I'll be in to check on you, James.' She kissed her brother's cheek and sent him off with Sami.

She took a clean glass from the bar, sat down beside Chris, and reached for the decanter. 'Sami. That awful cry.' She shivered and took a sip of brandy. 'I'll never forget it.'

'Dutch never thought of Sami, or anyone who lived in Cheneyville, or even most of his men, as anything other than expendable. The only things Sami brought away from Africa with him were his father's spear and his hatred of Dutch.'

'And it all came together here. If William had already set up a new life somewhere else, then that means he just wanted all of you dead.'

'Someone had to pay for his trouble. It was my fault that he only got half the bullion.

Because of me, Dutch, as William, had to work his holdings to maintain the lifestyle he'd imagined.' He hesitated. 'I suspected that he was in love with you, too, you know.'

Hearing that little word 'too,' she went into his arms, without hesitation but with a little cry of joy. He pulled her across his lap again and caught her to him in a crushing embrace.

'I have to take care of many details, and there will be questions from Marcos for all of us, but before I go, I want to tell you that you win. I admit it of my own free will. I want all you have to offer me, your heart, your mind, your body. When I saw Dutch touch you and heard the things he said to you, I feared losing you and your love more than I feared my own death. I realized that I love you more than life. I don't know what the future holds for us, Emily, but will you stay here at Abundancia? With me?'

She pulled back to look at him, tears in her eyes. Someday she'd tell him that she'd already decided to come to him on his terms, but not now, although she suspected he already knew because of what she'd just said to Sami. 'Yes, because I'm in love with you.'

Wrapped up in each other's arms and hearts, they misplaced the next few minutes. Emily was the first to recover.

Echoing his words from one of her first

nights at Abundancia, she said, 'We have a few details of our own to work out, and we won't get anywhere like this. I'll answer one of your questions, then you'll answer one of mine.'

'That sounds familiar. Are you suggesting another round of our peculiar version of Twenty Questions?'

'Yes, and I get to go first again. Are you sure you're ready to give up your bachelor ways? I've heard about Brazilian men and their women and mistresses. Trust is important to me, Chris. If you ever stray, I'll find out and I'll leave you. Do you understand me?'

He gasped and his tawny face paled. 'You'd do it, wouldn't you? I'll honor my promises to you. And you will honor yours to me,' he added in a voice that told her they both would. 'And that was two questions.'

'So it was. That was the most important thing I wanted to ask. And you're sure you can stand my chatter?'

'Ah, I know how to shut you up, remember?' He gave her a second, extended demonstration of this newfound ability.

It took her several minutes to get her breath back. 'When I disappear to Cornwall for a couple months of English summer each year, you'll understand that it has nothing to do with you or Abundancia?'

'I'll come with you. Holidays are important, and we'll have to keep James in line.'

'Okay, then how about this? My name is already established in my work, and I'll probably continue using Emily Noble for my illustrations. Will that bother you?'

'Hmm. If things work out, we'll hyphenate you sometime in the future. Emily Noble-Santos. It's even in keeping with your family's high aspirations: King, Noble, and Santos, meaning saints. Now stop hoarding all the questions. Are you sure you can work here?'

'I'm positive. I'll have to find a new publisher, but with a telephone, a fax, and a computer for communication, my work shouldn't be a problem. I'll have to go to New York a couple of times a year, though.'

'I can live with that. Are you sure you can stand the bad roads and the bad drivers here?'

'I'll let one of the men drive. Maybe Manoel. Being a one-eyed driver doesn't make any difference here.'

'Our Manoel is the best marksman of the lot. That's why I assigned him to you as your personal guard. Do you mind ex-military men working Abundancia?'

'No, I like those I've met very much. Will you teach me Portuguese? I want to learn all the dirty words first.'

'You mean those words I've been muttering under my breath since the moment you stumbled into my study? No problem. Anything else?'

'Yes. Will you please smoke less? I want you in excellent physical condition for many years to come.'

'I'll think about it. Offer me some incentive.'

'I'll tire you out with incentive. And you can think of every cigarillo you smoke as time off your life, time we could have made love.'

'You drive a hard bargain and you fight dirty.'

'Darn right. And can we lose the arsenal, the security cameras, and the monitors now that the danger is past? Your command center can be your hidey-hole when I'm driving you crazy.'

He brushed the line of her jaw with the backs of his fingers. 'Consider it done. But when you're driving me crazy, we'll work it out in the bedroom. I want to live with you in peace, Emily, for the rest of my days. Since I've admitted that, you'll be able to manipulate me shamelessly.'

She pushed her cheek against his hand, much like Gato, on the sofa behind her, was doing under her elbow at that very moment.

She reached back and stroked their cat briefly.

'What I offered you in Paulo's is part of my package deal, you know,' she whispered. 'You'll find refuge in my heart. Let my mind, such as it is, be your sanctuary. My body will give you peace. Are you sure you're up to possibly forever, Christovao of the *Cerrados?*'

Chris forged a trail of searing little kisses down her neck that sent sweet paralysis stealing through her mind. He didn't respond with words, but Emily knew his answer.

We do hope that you have enjoyed reading this large print book.

Did you know that all of our titles are available for purchase?

We publish a wide range of high quality large print books including:
**Romances, Mysteries, Classics**
**General Fiction**
**Non Fiction and Westerns**

Special interest titles available in large print are:
**The Little Oxford Dictionary**
**Music Book**
**Song Book**
**Hymn Book**
**Service Book**

Also available from us courtesy of Oxford University Press:
**Young Readers' Dictionary**
**(large print edition)**
**Young Readers' Thesaurus**
**(large print edition)**

For further information or a free brochure, please contact us at:
**Ulverscroft Large Print Books Ltd.,**
**The Green, Bradgate Road, Anstey,**
**Leicester, LE7 7FU, England.**
**Tel:** **(00 44) 0116 236 4325**
**Fax:** **(00 44) 0116 234 0205**